HOME FIRES

COMMON LAW BOOK FOUR

Kate Sherwood

D1273408

RIPTIDE
PUBLISHING

Riptide Publishing
PO Box 1537
Burnsville, NC 28714
www.riptidepublishing.com

Home Fires

Cover art: Natasha Snow, natashasnowdesigns.com
Editor: Carole-ann Galloway
Layout: L.C. Chase, lcchase.com/design.htm

ISBN: 978-1-62649-534-0

First edition
April, 2017

Also available in ebook:
ISBN: 978-1-62649-533-3

HOME FIRES

COMMON LAW BOOK FOUR

Kate Sherwood

RIPTIDE
PUBLISHING

TABLE OF
CONTENTS

CHAPTER 1

"Is there any possibility it's a practical joke?" Jericho Crewe asked. "Or just a rumor, maybe?"

Unfortunately, Sheriff Kayla Morgan shook her head. "I was the one who called them," she said, leaning back in her battered leather desk chair.

"You called the feds." Jericho waited a few seconds for the words to make sense, then gave up. "We have feds in town worrying about the border, feds in town still cleaning up the biker mess, feds in town investigating your dad, feds in town trying to catch Wade—and you woke up one morning, looked around, asked yourself, 'What does this town need more of?' and the answer you came up with was 'feds.' Honestly?"

Kayla's scowl suggested that Jericho wasn't the first person to express a similar opinion. "I'm not going to let my pride get in the way of doing my job, Jay. The FBI already knew about the basic situation—they're tracking about a dozen little militia groups in this part of the country—but they needed to know Tennant and his boys are flaring up. Receiving a big shipment of illegal weapons is definitely a break in their typical pattern of behavior."

"And you know that because you got an anonymous tip?" Jericho hated to do it. He didn't want to think it, much less say it. But . . . "Have you considered the possibility that this is more of Wade's bullshit? I mean, he—" Jericho's throat tightened as if the words shouldn't be spoken, but he was fairly used to his body betraying him when Wade was involved "—he was with me all weekend." Maybe Kay hadn't formally known that, but she wasn't clueless, and Jericho would be damned if he'd hide it. "So maybe this was just another case of him using me as an alibi, setting up something to distract everyone else, and then having one of his minions run a shipment across the border."

"I never thought I'd say this, Jay, but not every criminal activity in Mosely is connected to Wade Granger. Ninety-five percent of it, yeah. But I think this may have been something from that other five percent."

Jericho wanted to believe it. The weekend had been—well, not perfect, not considering the long car ride with two highly unpleasant children and then a lot more snakes than Jericho had ever wanted to see in one place—but it had been memorable, all the same. Jericho and Wade, outside of Mosely, weren't cop and criminal. They weren't their parents' sons, weren't men with painful histories, weren't running, and weren't refusing to run. They were just Jericho and Wade, and that was all they ever needed to be, as long as the world left them alone.

There had been nothing romantic about taking Jericho's half siblings on a road trip to the Billings zoo in order to fulfill Jericho's promise to get Elijah more access to snakes. Nothing romantic at all. And the two nights together had been fairly tame since Elijah and Nicolette had been sleeping in the adjoining motel room, but that hadn't mattered. It had still been Jericho and Wade in bed together, warm bodies and hot kisses, and Jericho was pretty sure he'd remember it all for the rest of his life.

They'd driven back the night before, dropped off the kids, and gone to Jericho's place as if it was the most natural thing in the world for them to stay together, and with no kids to worry about the night had been considerably hotter than the previous two. Then a late breakfast before Wade had left to do whatever Wade did all day and Jericho went for a run. Jericho hoped to be able to remember it as something pure, rather than as the latest episode of Wade's endless series of manipulations and games.

But Jericho was at work now, wearing the brown and beige polyester even if it was for one of the last times, and he needed to think like an under-sheriff, not a hormone-raddled teenager. "So if it wasn't Wade, who was it? Who do you think the tip was from?"

"Someone with knowledge of a single shipment of illegal weapons and ammo. So that means probably someone on the arms-dealer side, because it was only one shipment, no mention of the overall arsenal the militia has stockpiled."

"Or a disgruntled ex, or a neighbor who doesn't like the guys and wants to stir shit up. Might not be anything at all. The department's had an eye on these guys since well before I got here, and we've never seen anything to worry about before."

"Are you *negging* me, Jay? Is that what you're doing?" Kay frowned for a moment before her brows lifted in understanding. "Oh. You're worrying about how this is going to affect *you*. A bit harder to bail on me, guilt-free, if I'm in the middle of a big situation. Is that what you're thinking?"

Damn. Maybe it was. For too long Jericho had felt as if his life was out of his control, and he'd only recently started clawing it back. The weekend had been his announcement, to himself if no one else was listening, that the situation was going to change. But now? "*Is* it harder for me to bail out now? I mean, my reasons for quitting are the same as they were—I don't think I can be a good cop, the kind of cop I want to be, when I'm not sure I believe following the law is always the best idea, and—"

A shout from the main room interrupted his declaration. "We have agents down! Agents under fire, agents down!"

For a frozen half second, Jericho stared at Kayla, who stared back at him. Then they were both in motion, sprinting out to the central room.

The scene there was close to chaos. Federal agents and sheriff's deputies, all electrified and ready for action, desperately waiting for someone to tell them what to do.

The man on the phone, one finger plugging the ear he wasn't using to listen, was unfamiliar to Jericho, but his suit, haircut, and general attitude announced him as a fed. Almost certainly one of the new crop of FBI agents Kayla had invited into town. "Coldcreek Road," he told the crowd, but he spoke as if the words were in a foreign language. "Just past the canyon turnoff?"

And with that, half the room was in motion. The locals—and the feds who'd been around for a while—knew where they were going. The other half were pulling out their phones, tapping at them to call up the GPS.

Jericho let himself be washed along in the flow down the stairs. In LA, this all would have been different. There would have been a call to the SWAT team, a central command to coordinate squad cars and helicopters and snipers. But in Mosely, there was one M4 per squad car, and there were sidearms. That was all.

The feds wouldn't even have the M4s. Feds were good at stirring shit up, but they generally left the cleanup to special teams or locals. And the locals, officially, weren't too well armed, though if there'd been time, practically every deputy in the department could have run home to pick up a few hunting rifles or bigger stuff. But there was no time.

"Is this the militia?" Jericho demanded as he followed Kay to her squad car. "Coldcreek by the canyon turnoff—that's on the way to Tennant's place. Were there feds heading out there this afternoon?"

Her grim expression answered his question. A bunch of fanatics who'd just received a shipment of arms, and the sheriff's department was going after them with little more than cap guns and courage. "This is a federal operation," Jericho tried as Kayla wheeled the car out onto the street. "We don't actually *have* to get involved."

She kept her eyes on the road. "I can't hear you over the siren."

He leaned back in his seat. Shit. He was still wearing the brown and beige, and even if he hadn't been, he'd have followed Kayla wherever she led. So this was going to happen.

"Talk to dispatch, get things coordinated," Kayla ordered.

It would have made better sense for Jericho to have been driving so Kayla could do all that, but he did his best. As they raced through town and out into the mountains, he listened to the dispatchers sending back reports as they came in. Three feds injured, two others still active on-site. The feds were pinned down behind their vehicles, returning fire against an unknown number of perps who'd taken cover behind three cube vans. There was a more specific location, a helicopter was on the way, and someone was back at the dispatch center taking charge and directing units.

"Mosely County Five," the dispatcher called, and Jericho reached for the radio.

"County Five, go ahead," he said. Kayla kept her eyes on the road, but he could practically see her ears straining toward the radio.

"You're two klicks from a secondary road, no name on the map," the man at dispatch said. "It should lead around behind the incident. Break."

"Go ahead," Jericho barked. He hated radio protocols, but that was a fight for a different day. *Or for never*, he remembered. He was getting out of this policing business. The radio wouldn't be his problem soon. But already, that dream seemed to be receding.

"Assuming the road is passable, we're sending you and Mosely County Three down it. Circle the incident and block approaching traffic."

"We're not traffic cops," Kayla protested, but she wasn't holding the handset. If she had been, she probably wouldn't have said anything.

"Copy," Jericho confirmed, then ignored the radio as he scanned the road ahead. "See it?" he asked Kayla once he'd found the break in the trees.

"This is bullshit," she growled.

Of course she wanted to charge in with the rest of the team, wanted to be part of the action, wanted to prove she wasn't the local yokel the feds seemed to take them all for. But the car ahead of them was Mosely Three and it had its turn signal on. Kayla wouldn't leave any of her deputies without backup, and there was no time to argue with the assignments.

"Taking orders sucks," Jericho agreed as they bounced off the main road onto the much rougher path. Kayla didn't answer, so he busied himself with the GPS, then clicked on the radio handset. The road was so rutted he wished he had a third hand he could brace against the ceiling to steady himself. "Dispatch, County Five here. We're coming up on a spot that's really close to the active event. We could go cross-country on foot and get another angle on things."

Kayla glanced at him, clearly wanting to see the GPS and confirm his observation. But the car was still bouncing and jouncing and she was fighting to keep it on the road, which was more like a wide hiking trail.

"Copy, County Five," dispatch responded. "Stand by."

The wait was agonizing. "We're coming up on the best spot," Jericho told Kay.

"It's good?" she demanded. "This is a good path you're seeing?"

He crouched down to get a better view of the terrain out her side of the vehicle. "If it's passable, it's good. And it looks passable."

She reached over and flipped the siren on, just one long *meeeeeep*, the sound the department used to get the attention of other officers. Jericho was unlocking the M4 as Kay pulled them to a stop and by the time he had the ammo free of the glove box, she was out of the car, yelling instructions to the deputies, Meeks and— Shit. Meeks and Jackson.

Jericho hit the radio button. "Dispatch, County Three and Five are going cross-country. Advise other officers that we'll be on the slope above the event."

Outside the car, Jackson was arguing. "Dispatch directed us to—"

"I'm the sheriff," Kayla said calmly. No showdown, no getting in his face, just a simple reminder as she checked her gear and then started for the slope. His objections clearly weren't important enough for her to pay attention to. "Fall in."

Meeks and Jericho jogged up beside her, and they started into the woods.

Jackson was still back at the car, messing with the radio.

"Jackson, fall in *now*." Kayla barked.

He ignored her, holding on to the handset as if it were his route to salvation.

"Jackson, you're suspended from duty," Kayla said. "This is a restricted area. Remove yourself immediately—on foot, back along this road."

And then she turned to Jericho, her eyes a little brighter than usual, her cheeks flushed, but her voice still strong and level. "Jay, this is your area of expertise. You direct."

Too many tours of duty made that an unfortunate truth, and some part of Jay's mind had already been calculating, analyzing. The hill was steep, the ground covered in duff and debris that made them slide back half a step for every one they took forward. But all three of them were fit, and they were moving well.

"Shit." He sped up a little to get into the front. "I— Yeah, okay, but you guys tell me if you've got better ideas. I'll take point; you guys pick a flank. Keep your eyes open, let me know if you see anything."

That was all straightforward enough. "We'll have to get a better plan once we see what we're into."

That was when the sound of gunfire reached them. It was loud enough that Jericho knew the earlier silence had been because of a lull in the shooting, not because they'd been too far away to hear. He listened as he jogged up the hill, and his gut tightened. The noises were familiar, but after he got out of the military he'd hoped to never hear them again.

Automatic weapons, mixed in with a few single cracks, probably from the FBI agents' handguns. So at least one of them was still able to fire back. Jericho wondered how much ammunition an FBI agent would carry on a casual drive, and he picked up his pace until he was practically sprinting up the hill.

He was almost to the top when he sensed movement, just over the rise of the hill, off to the right.

Instinct and training made him drop to the ground, waving for the others to lower themselves behind him. Then he crawled forward, fast but careful. He eased his head around the side of a tree and his forehead burned, just as it always did in situations like this, as if his skin was anticipating the bullet. At least two inches of vulnerable skull had to be exposed before his eyes made it clear of the tree and he could see what was going on.

Three men. Unfamiliar, dressed in mismatched camo, carrying some serious firepower. Jesus, one of them had a fucking grenade launcher.

Jericho glanced behind him, saw Kay and Meeks only a yard or so away, and gestured for them to move sideways along the ridge, to the right. Toward the men, but as long as the team stayed quiet, the groups should pass each other without notice. And then Kay and Meeks would be behind the action, ready to step in as needed.

Hopefully.

Jericho waited as long as he could. He watched the three men striding forward—so confident, so oblivious. They were probably trying to circle around behind the agents below, hoping to take them out before reinforcements arrived. It was a reasonable strategy, but there was nothing else competent about them as they stomped through the forest; they seemed used to hunting things that didn't shoot back. Men who'd decided to play soldier, but who didn't want to follow the rules of being in the actual military.

Of course, stupid men were still dangerous, or maybe even *more* dangerous, when they were packing as heavy as these assholes were.

So Jericho took a deep breath and had his M4 ready before he half stepped out from behind the tree. "Mosely County Sheriff's Department," he barked. "Drop your weapons."

And as he'd known they would but prayed they wouldn't, the assholes swung their barrels up and toward him. He squeezed off a shot as he shifted back behind the tree. The guys had been five paces away, and Jericho had good aim; he didn't need to see the target's chest explode to know it had happened. But that left two assholes, and his tree wasn't the world's best cover.

Then Kayla shouted, "Freeze!" followed almost immediately by one shot, then another. Kayla's sidearm, Meeks's M4. Obviously the perps hadn't frozen.

Jericho spun back around his tree and found one of the targets with a bloody shoulder but still standing, still pointing his gun toward where Kayla and Meeks had returned to their sheltered position.

"Drop it," Jericho said. He tried to sound calmer than he had before, tried to make it apparent this was all over and there was no need to die for the cause. The only logical path forward was surrender.

Then Jericho's weird extra sense kicked into action, and he spun back behind his tree, crouched, edged around— *Shit.* There was someone coming toward them up the hill, and if Jericho moved to have cover from the new arrival, he'd be exposing himself to the wounded asshole. "Movement on our six!" Jericho bellowed. "Meeks, cover the injured perp. Morgan, cover Meeks against the new target."

Jericho flattened himself on the ground, making himself way less mobile than he wanted to be. He trained the barrel of his M4 back down the hill, pinpointed the movement, recognized the approaching figure—and was tempted to pull the trigger anyway.

"Drop it," he heard Meeks yell, and then the seemingly inevitable rattle of the M4 firing.

Then there was silence, even the gunfight below temporarily quiet, as Jericho glowered at Jackson struggling up the hill behind them.

The errant deputy saw Kayla, then shifted around so his back was to her and told Jericho, "We've been ordered to this position."

"No shit, asshole. Kay ordered us here." Jericho turned away, trying not to look at Jackson. Trying not to punch him in the face. Sure, maybe the third militia guy would have died anyway; maybe he would have stayed stupid, even if Jericho hadn't been distracted and had been able to keep trying to talk him down. But maybe not.

He turned to Kayla to see how she wanted to proceed, and found both her and Meeks staring at the bodies. Oh, shit. Things were usually pretty quiet in Mosely; it was entirely possible that neither of them had ever shot anyone before. Never taken a life, and never had to confront what their own bullets had done to a human who'd been alive only moments before.

"Forget it for now," he ordered them both. Things were still active, and they needed to stay on task. "Check your weapons and reload." *Stay busy, don't think. Don't look at what you just did, and don't start wondering who these guys were, what brought them here, or how else you could have handled the situation. Don't think about who's at home waiting for them, and who's going to be at their funerals.* Those thoughts would all come to anyone who hadn't lost all humanity, but they couldn't come while you were still in the field.

Jericho kept his weapon ready as he eased toward the three bodies. There was no doubt about their status, but training was training, and there could be other enemies nearby.

He crouched by the first man, the one who'd been carrying the grenade launcher. The sounds of the firefight flared up again, and this time Jericho was relieved to hear the three-round burst of the sheriff's department's M4s. The cavalry had arrived. But they would still be woefully underpowered if the gear on these three was typical. Jericho started working the weapons off the dead body as he turned and told Jackson, "Run back down the hill and tell dispatch we have three bad guys down. One M32 in our custody, with—" Jericho jerked the man over and poked into his backpack "—12 HE rounds." He surveyed the other bodies and added, "M4 with an M203, double-barreled shotgun, couple handguns—"

He broke off as Jackson moved closer and poked one of the bodies with the toe of his boot.

Somehow, it was that gesture that made Jericho's rage explode. "Get the fuck away from him, you insubordinate coward!" He was about to say something about Jackson not *deserving* to touch one of the men someone else had killed, but he caught himself in time. They weren't hunters, and the fallen weren't trophies. They were human beings, or had been, and there was no damn reason for anyone to be kicking them. Instead he stepped forward, brought his face to within an inch of Jackson's, and growled, "Get your ass down the hill. Report in as ordered. And don't come back up. Is that fucking clear?"

Jackson's eyes widened. Jericho knew why. The deputy was used to living in the safe, respectful civilian world, where his politics and connections made a difference. But up here, at this moment?

"You've been suspended," Jericho said. "And you came up the hill anyway and messed up our operation. The only reason you're not sitting there cuffed to a goddamn tree is that you *might* be useful if you follow your fucking orders. So get moving or turn around and give me your wrist."

"Yeah, you'd like it if I turned around," Jackson sneered.

It was so stupid. So petty, so childish, so absurd. Right up there on the mountain, with three dead bodies at his feet and a firefight raging down the hill, Jericho laughed out loud. Mostly in surprise, and maybe a bit of extra aggression mixed in.

"Jesus, Jackson," Kay said, shaking her head. "Don't give me any *more* reasons to fire you. Get your ass down the goddamn hill."

Jackson had his eyes narrowed and his mouth open, never a good combination for him, when Meeks urgently said, "Go, Jack. Shit. Just go."

And finally Jackson started moving.

The whole exchange had been quick, maybe fifteen seconds, and Jericho was pretty sure it had been worthwhile. Dispatch needed to know about the grenade launcher, if nothing else. But, still, he felt guilty for wasting time. A lot of rounds could be fired in fifteen seconds, a lot of bullets that could do a lot of damage to human bodies. Feds' bodies, and deputies' too.

"Let's move," Jericho said, gesturing to the right. "Back to the original plan. We'll try get in behind them, like their guys were trying to do to ours."

Then they were off again, a shuffling run that had all of Jericho's muscles singing a familiar song. The adrenaline, the mix of fear and relief, the savage triumph he was almost ashamed of but couldn't deny. For a moment, he thought of Wade. Was the difference between them just that Wade was more *honest* about the things Jericho tried to hide? Wade embraced his darkness just as surely as his light, and there was something about that—

Something that Jericho couldn't think about in the middle of a goddamn combat situation! Shit, he was losing it.

He sped up a little, heard Meeks grunting in exertion, heard Kayla's breathing, heavy but controlled. It was important for him to keep his mind on the job for their sakes as much as his own.

So he got his brain working, let his awareness spread as it always did in combat, no focus, only a blur of *everything*. No time to study any details when all he needed was the general classification of dangerous or not dangerous.

They moved fast along the ridge for a few hundred yards before Jericho started angling down. There was still sporadic fire from below, and he checked his watch. Less than thirty minutes since the call had come in. Not enough time to get a helicopter to them, apparently, but it must have felt like a damn lifetime for the agents below. Maybe literally their lifetime.

Jericho dropped low and let himself skid down the slope, sending duff and pebbles tumbling below. He had a better view now, and could see how the situation was laid out. The road was narrow, with a slope up on one side, a slope down on the other. Three cube vans blocked the road in one direction, and about a hundred yards in the other direction there were the original two fed sedans, shot up almost beyond recognition, and behind that a stream of cruisers, sedans, and ambulances. The problem was that the terrain was so linear. There was no room for law enforcement to spread out and put their greater numbers to work. At least, there was no room for that on the lower level. But Jericho's team was up high.

They worked forward, worked sideways, and then he found it. The spot wasn't perfect; there were a couple of trees obscuring parts of the militia line. But it was good. Definitely good enough.

"Rifles shoot, handgun covers shooters," he hissed to the other two. He didn't care who did which job, but the division of labor was common sense. They were about two hundred yards from the militia, well beyond the effective range of a sidearm. He was tempted to break out the grenade launcher, but something in him just couldn't do it. Grenades were for Afghanistan, not for the United States. Not for Mosely.

"Trade," Kayla said, and he heard her and Meeks shuffling around as he found a good firing position. Kayla wasn't a great shot, but she was fine, and he had the feeling she might be taking the gun as a way to take the responsibility; Meeks was still looking pretty shaky after the previous engagement. He might not be ready to pull the trigger again, and Kayla probably wanted to spare him from making the decision.

And Kay was solid. Gray-faced and wide-eyed, but Jay knew to his core that she wouldn't let it slow her down.

"Okay," he said quietly as she settled beside him. "I've spotted seven perps. If they stay under cover, we just observe, but as soon as one of them pops up to fire, we take him out. If two come up at the same time, you take the one on the left. If more than two, you start left and work in, I'll start right and do the same."

Her nod was jerky, but clear.

They didn't have to wait long. There was a signal from one of the militia members, and all of them rose at once, practically brazen from Jericho's perspective, poking their guns around the vehicles they were using for cover—

Jericho's shot came a fraction of a second before Kay's. Two men fell, and the others stood frozen, confused. Jericho's second shot found its target, and he was lined up for his third before Kay fired. By then, the militia was moving, scrambling, and Kay's bullet hit the side of the van where a perp had been a second earlier. They were yelling as they crowded inside the vans, hoping for whatever shelter could be offered by a bit of sheet metal, and Jericho didn't want to think about them in there, sitting in the dark, waiting for the bullets that would pierce the metal, then their bodies.

Jericho needed direction. He wasn't a leader, wasn't good at being in charge. He'd risk his own life, but hated the idea of risking someone else's. "Disable the vans, or let them get away?" he asked Kay.

She didn't answer for a full breath, out and in, and then said, "Fuck. No, the bastards shot federal agents. It'd be easier to let them disengage, but then they'd be out there."

So she took her aim and Jericho took his. They focused on the tires and the engine block, creating explosive destruction that would have been fun if he hadn't been far too aware of the human lives protected by the thin van walls.

When all the tires were flat and the engines steaming, Jericho checked his ammo and passed an extra clip to Kay while keeping his eyes on the scene below. "Okay. I think I can hear the helicopters. We can give cover so the ambulances can make it in and pick up our guys." He saw her grim nod out of his peripheral vision. "So, essentially, our work here is done. Would now be a good time for us to talk about my resignation?"

CHAPTER 2

The cleanup hadn't gone as tidily as Jericho might have wished, but within a couple of hours the remaining militia members at the ambush site had been teargassed out of their vans, disarmed by a flown-in special team complete with gas masks and full-body armor, and then cuffed and transported.

Of course, there was still a lot of reporting and paperwork to go through once they were back at the station. There was always paperwork. The crime scene investigators took the M4 Jericho had used in order to do ballistic tests. They also took his sidearm, even though he hadn't fired it. Being unarmed left him feeling a bit naked and unbalanced. Hell, maybe that had been their goal.

The feds were in charge of the whole show, so Jericho spent most of his time answering their questions and repeatedly walking them through his team's actions on the hillside. The agents were more respectful than he was used to, almost friendly. Amazing how people's attitudes changed when you helped them rescue their colleagues from insane militiamen.

"What was their goal?" he asked when the last round of activity had died down and it was his turn to ask some questions. It was pushing midnight, and the feds had taped off a couple hundred acres of mountain land as a crime scene. Montgomery and Hockley were sitting with Jericho and Kayla, since the FBI didn't seem to want DEA help any more than they'd wanted the sheriff's department to be involved. And it had been kind of sweet to see Hockley and Kay give each other a quick, worried once-over, each ensuring the other's health without making a big scene about it. Kayla had told Jericho that Hockley was an *ex*-lover, but maybe she'd been playing up the *ex*. Regardless, they were cute, and it was tempting to comment on it. Then Jericho thought back to the mess on the mountain and his mood darkened.

"They couldn't have seen that going down differently, could they?" Jericho asked the little band. "The militia. I mean, they did some damage, sure, but even if they'd won that fight, they had to know the federal government wasn't going to walk away and let it go. Why the hell did they start this?"

The others didn't seem to have any better answers than Jericho did, and the four of them sat quietly for a while. Jericho was summoning some final energy reserve to get him off his chair and home when there was a shuffling sound on the stairs and everyone in the office turned to see Wade Granger's head appear. He froze as soon as he saw Jericho, five or six steps from the top, and his face was—damn, it was prime Wade, with about a dozen different emotions playing across it simultaneously. But this time, the emotions seemed genuine, and if that was true, if Wade was stretched so far that he was showing that kind of vulnerability in the damn sheriff's office—

Jericho stood up slowly, and Wade was gone. His footsteps were audible, not running but almost, as he left. Jericho stared after him.

"Did you not call him?" Kayla asked, her voice hushed in disbelief. "He would have heard about all this—and you didn't call him to say you were okay?"

"I—" Jericho had no idea what to say, and of course it wasn't Kay he should be saying it to anyway. "Shit."

He moved fast, to the stairs in two long strides, descending in a sort of controlled fall, and then across the lobby and out the front doors without paying any attention to who else was there, who was seeing him. No one else mattered.

Once outside, Jericho scanned the parking lot desperately. He dug in his pocket for his phone, then saw the shadows move and an interior light switch on as someone opened the door of a pickup at the far end of the parking lot.

"Wade," Jericho yelled, loud enough he'd certainly been heard. But Wade didn't turn, didn't respond in any way; he just stood there staring into the truck.

Jericho broke into a jog, only slowing when he was a couple of steps away. "Wade," he said cautiously. "I'm sorry. I didn't think—"

That was as far as he got before Wade spun, grabbed Jericho by his shirt, and slammed him into the side of the pickup next to his. "You didn't think," Wade growled. One forearm shifted across Jericho's throat, holding him in place, while the other roamed desperately over Jericho's body—frisking him? No, checking for damage.

Jericho was bigger than Wade, better trained than Wade—if they were actually fighting, Jericho would win. But they weren't fighting, not really.

"I thought about you today, just like I always do," Jericho admitted. His voice was a little strained as it worked past the pressure on his throat. "But it didn't occur to me that you'd be worried. I'm sorry."

"You didn't think I'd be worried?" Wade demanded. His hands had stopped moving, now, one still across Jericho's throat, the other gripping his belt. "All day long I'm hearing about a fucking shoot-out, seeing choppers coming and going, everyone going crazy, and I can't call you, can't come see whether you're okay, because I'd just be feeding the feds more fucking reasons to not trust you, and all I can do is sit there and imagine all the reasons why you can't let me know what's going on. So I come up with a stupid fucking cover story, an excuse to let me get inside the department and at least see what's going on, and I go up the stairs and you're having a fucking tea party?" His voice broke, and he took a deep breath, then brought both hands to Jericho's shoulder and shoved, hard. "You're a fucking asshole, Crewe."

"I thought you'd know," Jericho said. It was a bit lame, maybe, but it was true. "You know everything that happens in this town before anybody else does, *including* everything that happens at the sheriff's station or with the feds. I thought you'd know about this."

"I didn't," Wade said. For a moment it seemed like he was going to let it go; Jericho could almost feel the tension in Wade's body starting to drain away. But then Wade shoved Jericho again, just as hard, and said, "This is bullshit. I'm not going to do this, not going to sit around worrying about you when I know I can't do a single fucking thing to help. No, Jay. If you're going to do dangerous shit, you need to do it *with me* so I know what's happening, so I can do something about it."

Jericho sighed. "I'm not a kid anymore. I'm not *looking* to do dangerous things. But today? There was no choice, Wade. Kay was going in, and I—"

"Fucking Kay! Jesus, Jericho, she's a grown-ass woman, and she's the fucking sheriff. She doesn't need you babysitting her. I'm sick of hearing about her, and how you have to do shit because of her. You *don't* have to. You don't owe her a goddamn thing."

"She's a friend, and things are tough right now. Someone's got to have her back."

"She's got her fed friends for that, doesn't she?"

"Jesus, Wade, are you fucking *jealous*? Kay needed help, and even if she hadn't, there were officers under fire. *They* needed help."

"And you had to be one of the people helping them. It had to be your problem." Wade shook his head. Now the tension was leaving him for real, and Jericho almost wished it would come back, because anger was better than this unfamiliar, defeated Wade it was leaving behind. "And if it's your problem, it's my problem," Wade said. It sounded almost like he was talking to himself. "Goddamn it." Then he looked up, eyes bright and hard. "You're not quitting the job. Right? All that talk on the weekend was just talk—just fucking make-believe."

"It wasn't just talk," Jericho said, but he had to add, "Not when I was saying it. But now? *Right* now? I can't walk away from this, Wade. It's not just Kayla who needs me—Jackson's gone from half-assed whiner to full-on insubordination, the other deputies are either too old to do field work or too young to keep themselves alive without help. We've got dead feds and dead militia assholes and a hell of a mess all round. I can't quit—not yet." He tried to catch Wade's gaze, but the man had gone back to looking at the ground. "I'm sorry, but I can't."

They stood quietly for a few moments, and then Wade raised his head and smiled. "Of course not." He sounded calm and reasonable, and that was never good. "I understand. You have commitments."

"Wade," Jericho said warningly. Whatever plan was being developed, whatever trap was being set, he didn't want any part of it.

But Wade just leaned forward and gave him a quick kiss, then stepped back toward his pickup. "Sorry for interrupting your work. You should get back inside." There wasn't even a hint of venom in his voice when he added, "Kayla needs you."

"Shit, Wade." Jericho didn't have any other words, couldn't hope to outthink Wade. All he had was his sincerity, and compared to Wade's deviousness it didn't seem like much of a tool. Still, he tried.

He reached for Wade, found the warm skin of his neck and tugged him forward. He was too pliant, too cooperative, but it was Wade somewhere in there, and Jericho kissed him with as much sweetness as he could find, as much need and apology and truth and tenderness. And, eventually, Wade kissed him back, and maybe that was enough.

But it was Wade who pulled away first. "This is the sheriff's parking lot, Jay. Not the time or place."

"I'm not going to hide it. Seriously, the feds know, the deputies know, and I'm not doing anything illegal. If you want to call me during the day to see if I'm okay? Call me. I don't care who's listening in. Fuck them. If you want to come by my place? Come by. We'll wave at the surveillance team before we close the curtains and ignore them. Okay?"

"And what about darling Kay?" Wade asked with raised eyebrows. "How's that going to look? Corrupt father *and* corrupt under-sheriff—"

"I'm not corrupt," Jericho said firmly. "If you come by, it's personal. I'm not going to feed you information from work, and if you tell me something—well, if you tell me something I'll assume it's another piece in whatever trap you're currently building and I'll try to figure out how to disarm the damn thing, but I'll pass it along to Kay and the feds, just like I've been doing all along. I'm not offering to get in bed with you in any but a literal sense."

"And the county voters will absolutely understand that."

"That'll be Kay's problem. If she wants to fire me, she can. But I've already told her—or at least I started to—if it comes down to choosing between you and my job, I choose you."

"Yeah?" Wade's smile was a little softer this time, a little more real. "Damn, Junior, you can be a real sweet-talker when you try to be."

"Don't get too worked up," Jericho said, letting his hands fall to Wade's waist. "I really don't like my job very much."

Wade grinned, and Jericho kissed him, and they were good again. Sure, Wade was still going to scheme and plan, but that was okay. It wouldn't be Wade if he weren't doing that, and anything that wasn't Wade? Jericho wasn't interested.

"Do you need to go back inside?" Wade asked.

Jericho shook his head. "I don't think so. I'll call Kay and tell her I'm leaving. And you should know that she thought I was an asshole for not calling you earlier and letting you know I was okay. You might not be her favorite person, but—"

"But she's happy to have an excuse to bitch at you and try to scold you back into the fold of respectable behavior and domestication."

Jericho didn't respond to that; there was no point. Instead, he texted Kayla that he was taking a break and would be back first thing, asked her to keep him in the loop if there were new developments, then turned to Wade. "I know I said it doesn't matter, but just in case you were still feeling shy? I don't think there's a fed in this quarter of the continent working on anything but the militia case. If you came back to my place with me, there wouldn't be anyone jotting it down in their logbook."

"Well, I wasn't wrong about you being a sweet-talker, was I?" Wade's smile seemed real, but a little sad. "So, yeah. I'll come with you." He took a step backward toward his truck. "That's what's going to get me in trouble, isn't it?"

Jericho woke to his phone ringing, fumbled for it, stabbed blindly at the screen, and managed to bring it to his ear. "Crewe," he mumbled.

"I want you at an all-agency meeting at eight," Kayla told him without preamble. "I've been up all night and my brain's fried, so I need someone else there to pick up on anything I miss."

He fought for consciousness. "Eight? What time is it now?"

"Seven thirty."

Of course it was. Jericho shifted around to sit more-or-less upright and plant his feet on the floor, and only then did he realize that his mattress felt different. His blankets weren't moving like they normally would. He peered over his shoulder, and Wade was there, lying on his back, one arm behind his head, looking up at Jericho with bright, alert eyes. Jericho blinked, then smiled. Wade was in his bed, where he belonged. The day before had been a mess, but things had turned around as soon as Wade appeared.

"So you'll be here?" Kayla prompted.

"Might be a bit late. Save a cup of coffee for me." Then Jericho ended the call, bent over and kissed Wade's bare shoulder, nibbled up toward his neck—and was pushed away with a firm hand.

"You need to go to work," Wade said.

"Since when do you care about my attendance record?" Jericho said, and tried to lean back in.

But Wade held him at bay. "I don't care when you're doing the caring for us. But when you stop caring, somebody has to step in, so I guess it'll have to be me."

It was sweet, in a way, thinking of them as that much of a team. But also stupid and frustrating. "What about if we just both didn't care? Is there a reason we can't do that?"

Wade's smile was fond, but patronizing. "How many times have you flip-flopped on all this since you got back here? If you want me to believe you really don't care about your job, then you need to keep not caring about it for a period of time. A couple weeks at least. But until then, you're on don't-care probation, and that means you shouldn't be allowed to screw things up too bad, in case you change your mind and want to go back to being a good little officer."

"I don't actually think it's your job to babysit me like that."

"Oh. So I'm not allowed to tell you things about your job, like that you should get there on time, but you can tell me about my job?"

"Babysitting me *isn't* your job."

"I'm self-employed." Wade leaned back into his pillows, clearly satisfied. "My job is whatever I say it is."

Jericho lurched off the bed, not worrying about how he might be jouncing Wade. "Fine. I don't want to mess around with you anymore anyway."

"Yeah, you do," Wade said, but Jericho refused to turn around and see his smug grin. He just stalked off to the shower, climbed in, sudsed up his face and hair with the same generic bodywash—and then felt a draft of cool air as the shower curtain shifted.

"Have you never seen *Psycho*?" he demanded, still facing the wall in front of him. "Do you really think it's a good idea to sneak up on people in the shower?"

"I think it's a great idea." Wade's breath was cool against the shower-heated skin of Jericho's neck. "Turn around."

"What happened to your concern about my attendance record?" Jericho asked as he turned, his body wet and slick against Wade's.

"I decided I could be quick. I'll have you coming and then going inside five minutes."

Jericho's cock was already hardening, straining toward Wade, but he felt as if he should protest on principle. "I'm not that out of control."

"No?" Wade raised an eyebrow, confident and beautiful. "Count to three hundred. One-steamboat, two-steamboat style."

"Three hundred?"

"That's five minutes." Wade kissed Jericho's jawline, then growled, "Count."

And god help him, Jericho counted. He was in the twenties as Wade slid down his body, in the forties, with his voice rising a little as Wade teased, licked, sucked just the head of his cock. By sixty Wade's mouth surrounded him, hot and wet and demanding, and of course there was an extra flick of his tongue at sixty-nine.

Jericho leaned back, bracing his shoulders on the cool ceramic tiles, and tried to think about the numbers, not what Wade was doing with his tongue, his lips, his hands. "Ninety-two," he gasped as Wade slid a finger past his balls, up the crack of his ass, and then eased inside. And that was the end of any shred of subtlety or restraint. Wade's mouth and finger synchronized for a full-on assault against Jericho's self-control and the numbers got even trickier to keep track of.

"Fuck it," Jericho managed when he stumbled over one forty seven. He wasn't going to last to anywhere near three hundred, and he was way too far gone to worry about his lack of stamina. When he needed to stay hard, he could stay— Oh Jesus, Wade's free arm wrapped around Jericho's waist, tugging him closer, holding him, restraining him, and there was a second finger added to his ass, a moment of burn and stretching before they found their target together, and Jericho was done.

"Fuck," he groaned, and then louder, "Fuck, Wade. Wade. Wade!"

And he let himself go. Wade hummed his triumphant approval, eased off enough to make swallowing easier, and kept working his fingers, demanding more from Jericho's body, which was already so willing to give so much.

Jericho was slumped back against the tiles, only dimly aware of the water still falling on his chest, when Wade slithered up his body. "I win," Wade said, and there was a moment of perfection before he pulled away and shoved Jericho's shoulders, adding, "You need to get in gear, Junior! You've got a meeting to attend."

Jericho wanted to stay in the shower, definitely for a lot longer, possibly forever, but he made himself climb out and towel himself off. Wade got out too, but didn't bother with getting dry or putting clothes on. He just wandered to the kitchen and started puttering, and by the time Jericho was dressed in his goddamn awful beige polyester uniform, there was a beautiful naked man waiting by the apartment door with a travel mug of coffee and a toasted PB&J.

"Wow," Jericho said cautiously. It was obviously a trap, and he was probably already completely entangled. "You are being really, *really* generous today. What's up?"

Wade arched an eyebrow. "I'm feeling benevolent. Don't get used to it."

"I won't." A quick kiss, then a longer one, then a mug of coffee pressing against Jericho's chest, Wade's other hand shoving him toward the door.

"You're up to something," he said as he stepped outside. Wade gave him a beatific smile and shut the door in his face.

There's nothing in the apartment he shouldn't see, Jericho told himself as he headed for the car. Nothing in Jericho's *life* Wade shouldn't see. His laptop was sitting in the car beside him, and he didn't have any department files at home. So snooping wasn't a worry. But that didn't mean Wade wasn't up to something.

Of course, Wade was always up to something, and there was never any chance Jericho would figure it out, so he might as well give up and get on with his day.

There were reporters outside the sheriff's building, with TV vans from the big networks and a couple of deputies looking a bit intimidated as they tried to keep the press contained. Jericho stopped the car beside Watson, a first-year deputy who spent most of his time writing traffic tickets for tourists.

"You doing okay?" Jericho asked without a glance toward the cameramen panning toward him. He'd worked enough murder cases in LA to know that the press should be ignored any time they weren't being used.

"They're saying this is a national story," Watson whispered, eyes wide. "They're filming stuff they're going to show all over the country."

Feds and militias? Yeah, that always got attention. "Make sure they get your good side," he suggested. "And keep them off the lawn. It's in bad shape as it is."

"Yes, sir," Watson answered, clearly wondering which was his good side. Jericho pulled into the parking lot.

He arrived at the briefing with moments to spare and snuck around the back of the room to stand behind Kay's seat. There were about thirty people crowded into the station's only conference room, most of them familiar, some not. And as he glanced around at their faces his light mood sank to the pit of his stomach. Sheriff's department and state police were present, but everyone else was federal, mostly FBI. There were agents with tear-red eyes, agents with jaws so tight they looked like they were trying not to scream, and at the front of the room, an agent with his arm in a sling glowering like an avenging angel rather than a beat-up fed.

"Let's get started," he said, his voice a low rumble. He was a big man, maybe ten years older than Jericho, and he gave the impression of someone who didn't take crap from anyone. "I'm Lawrence Casey, Special Agent in Charge. I was one of the men injured yesterday, so I haven't been a part of this investigation since the shooting. But I'm back now."

There was a murmur, not of voices but of movement, as the agents in the room shifted. Jericho couldn't figure out if the reaction was favorable or not.

"We lost two good agents yesterday, Kanwal and Foster, and Agent Hill remains in the hospital. The long delay before evacuation contributed to the seriousness of her injuries, but a full recovery is—" He stopped, swallowed hard, as if the formal words weren't quite enough to cover his emotions, then continued. "A full recovery is to be hoped for."

There was a moment of quiet in the room. Then Casey said, "Six suspects were killed at the scene of the incident, and we have four more in custody." He looked back and his gaze found Kayla, then Jericho.

"It was good work from our local colleagues that ended the standoff," he acknowledged, and Jericho had to push down a swelling of pride. There was no reason to celebrate, not with so many people dead, but yeah, damn it, it *had* been good work.

He kept his game face on and Kay did too, and after a moment Casey nodded at them and went on with his briefing.

Jericho stood and listened and tried to understand. The militia had barely been a blip on the radar before this. He'd visited Sam Tennant, the head of the group, on a few occasions himself, just checking in and making the police presence known. Tennant was a heavily bearded, camo-wearing good ol' boy who didn't care too much about things like hunting licenses or keeping his cars properly registered and insured, but that was a good description of half the population of Mosely County. Jericho had been sworn at and then run off the property every time he'd visited, but Sam had always seemed harmless enough as he brandished his shotgun and bellowed about his rights. He made a lot of noise, but never anything more; it might have looked bad from the outside, but it was a hell of a big step from yelling to laying a damn ambush and opening fire.

And Tennant hadn't been one of the men at the shoot-out the day before—not one of the bodies, not one of the arrested men. But he was being discussed in this meeting like some sort of political reactionary, not just an antisocial redneck. The feds were thinking of him as a dangerous man.

"The arms shipment has been confirmed, and we're tracking down more information from the supply side," Casey told the room. "But based on what we saw yesterday and what we've discovered so far, we need to assume these guys are heavily armed and absolutely ready to use their weapons." He scanned the crowd as if checking to be sure his message was being given proper weight, then continued. "We've got surveillance on the compound now and the access road is securely blockaded. We're going to take our time with this and do it right."

"That property's five miles from the border, wooded most of the way," Jericho said. "Have you warned the Canadians we might be flushing a few Long-Bearded Rednecks into an early migration?"

And just like that, Casey's expression grew dour. Apparently he was happy to have locals do his shooting for him, but not so happy when they questioned his plans. "When I say we've got surveillance in place, I don't mean a lone deputy in a squad car. The federal government has resources beyond those you'd be accustomed to, and we've brought them to bear in this case."

"Yeah? So, what've you got? Some telecom stuff, maybe multilateration to track the phones? Doesn't work that well when there's only one tower in range, but it's a start. Maybe UAVs, hopefully with infrared options. Satellites? You got one going geo-sync on this? That'd be nice. All that stuff is great, but when it comes down to it, information doesn't do you much good unless you can act on it. And if those boys head out their back doors and start walking north, what exactly can you do? The forest is too dense to land a chopper—you got agents trained to be paratroopers? They sitting at the airport right now? Because once the boys go, you'll have less than an hour to intercept before they're across the border and everything gets ten times more complicated." Jericho shrugged. "Unless you're ready to carpet bomb a few hundred acres of American soil, catching these guys before they hit the border would be like catching a mosquito with a teaspoon. In the dark."

"So what's your point, Under-sheriff?"

"My point? Well, I started with a question. I wanted to know if you've contacted the Canadians—have you?"

"We've shared preliminary information," Casey bit out. "An extended briefing will likely be forthcoming."

Jericho smiled peacefully. "Okay, then. That's all I was asking about."

Casey gave him a stare, then said, "We have a team on the way to deal with communication and negotiations. We have another team that will handle the interrogation of the men in custody. Our plan is to pursue criminal charges against those involved in the incident yesterday while continuing our investigation of those not directly involved. Yesterday was an unexpected tragedy, but we have regrouped and will proceed with care and attention to detail."

He paused, looked around the room, then added, "The FBI appreciates the support offered by other agencies yesterday, at the federal, state, and local levels. But it was only necessary because we hadn't anticipated this level of resistance. Now that we know what we're dealing with, we will be carrying on using FBI resources. This is the last all-agency meeting we have scheduled. Thank you, everyone, for your help."

Jericho let himself glance over at Hockley, sitting with his DEA buddies, and the frustration on their faces was almost enough to make it worthwhile. Sure, the sheriff's department was getting pushed out of *another* case on their turf, but this time the DEA was getting pushed out too. Now Hockley had some idea how it felt.

Then Hockley noticed Jericho's attention, obviously recognized it for what it was, and gave him a rueful grin. Damn. Jericho might actually find himself liking the son of a bitch.

"My office," Kayla told Jericho quietly, and she made eye contact with Hockley and nodded gently toward the exit. Time to go get some real work done.

Jericho fell in behind his boss, pausing only to jab his pen through the middle of four donuts on the table by the door, then strode on, carrying his baked goods like a trophy. When he reached Kay's office he offered her one, took one for himself, then turned and held the pen out to Hockley and Montgomery, who were standing in the doorway.

"Welcome to the Outcasts Club," he said. "We have snacks, but only if we pilfer them from the overlords."

"Don't drag us into your fantasy world," Montgomery said, but he took a donut, and then a seat. Jericho settled his ass on the windowsill so Hockley could take the other free chair.

"They have no local contacts," Hockley said, clearly more interested in bitterness than sweets. "They don't know the terrain. They won't know what's normal up here and what's worth investigating." He turned to Jericho. "You were right about the border, obviously. But the FBI isn't stupid—they can look at a map and see the problem." He sighed. "I'm just not sure what they're going to do about it."

"Maybe they don't need to do *anything*," Jericho tried. "Do we really believe Sam Tennant or any of his boys were behind yesterday's mess? I mean, the feds—the FBI, sorry—they're thinking of Sam as the leader. But yesterday was a deliberate shoot-out with federal agents; Sam's a jackass, but he's not that stupid or that crazy, is he? So maybe it'd be okay if the FBI ignores the border, and Sam and his less-than-crazy friends slip across. He can hang out up north for a while until things get figured out down here."

"You think we should just let him walk? I mean, if it wasn't Sam, who was it?" Kayla asked. "Who *is* stupid or crazy enough to try something like this?"

"Have you guys not seen the internet this morning?" Montgomery asked with a frown.

Jericho shivered at the memory of what *he'd* been doing instead of checking his email, and caught a furtive glance between Hockley and Kay—maybe they'd been similarly distracted?

"What's on the internet?" Hockley asked his partner.

"A call to arms. Some hard-core whack job based in Idaho named Lucas Templeton, saying this is the final federal aggression that he and his followers are going to tolerate. According to them, this was an *FBI* ambush and the militia members only fought back because they knew they'd have been murdered otherwise. Self-defense."

"Okay, that's somebody capitalizing on the situation," Kay said. "But you aren't actually suggesting that was the original motivation, are you? You aren't saying they did it on purpose, to be martyrs?"

Montgomery shrugged. "I'm not saying, but I'm wondering."

"Why would they come all the way up here?" Hockley mused. "Why not stay in Idaho?"

"Maybe the border," Jericho said. "I don't want to sound obsessed, but it's why you guys spend so much time here, right? It's why this town is still alive after the mine closed down—smuggling shit across that imaginary line is good business. But it'd also be a pretty good escape route. I'm not saying the Mounties wouldn't do their part and help out, but they're not going to spend the kind of man hours on it that we would. And every time someone pops across the border, whoever's chasing them, from one side or the other, has to fall back."

"I remember my dad bitching about you doing that, years ago," Kayla said. There was an awkward moment as her expression showed that she'd remembered what was happening with her dad, remembered why she didn't talk about him at work anymore. But then she raised her chin and charged on. "You and Wade, being stupid, and he and Garron chasing you and you'd run north across the border, then turn around and run south as soon as you thought you were clear."

"Or as soon as we wanted more attention, more of an adrenaline rush," Jericho said. "God, we were assholes. I'm surprised they didn't shoot us."

"Me too." Kayla shook her head ruefully. "Maybe your actual parents didn't care what you two got up to, but you had me worried sick."

"Sorry," Jericho said. It wasn't really enough. "Like I said—we were assholes."

Montgomery had his mouth open to make a comment, probably about Jericho's use of the past tense, but Hockley cut in with, "Okay, let's get back to the current issue. We—well, Jericho, and I assume other members of the sheriff's department—have an existing relationship with one of the chief suspects in the current clusterfuck. The sheriff's department also has significant knowledge of the local terrain, and the local culture in general. The FBI is either unaware of these assets or simply isn't interested in taking advantage of them. So, the question is, what are we going to do about that?"

"If we pooled our resources, I bet we could buy a farm in some third-world country. We could move down there and live like kings," Jericho suggested.

"Let's keep that as a plan B," Kayla said.

Then there was a knock on the door and everyone's gaze shifted. Deputy Garron shoved the door open and lumbered inside, closed the door behind him, frowned at Hockley and Montgomery, then told Kayla, "Jenny Taylor's outside. She's got Butch Travis with her and Ben Tran." Garron sounded like he was delivering notice of an execution order when he added, "Jackson's with them."

A county commissioner, a justice of the peace, the editor of the city's weekly newspaper, and the disaffected deputy who knew Kayla's father was being investigated for corruption. "This is not the fucking time—" Jericho started, but Kayla raised her hand to cut him off.

"When *is* the time?" Her smile only seemed a little forced as she told the others, "I need to deal with this. Could you continue the meeting in Jericho's office?"

"Hell no," Jericho said. "We should stay. At least I should."

"If Jackson's with them, we've already got one more loose cannon than necessary. I don't think having two will make anything better."

"Kay . . ."

"Jay. I've got this. It's not going to convince them that I'm fit to be sheriff if I have to get backup just to talk to a few concerned citizens."

"It's your dad being investigated, not you."

"And I will certainly point that out to them if they seem to be confused. But I'll do it on my own." She raised her eyebrows and nodded toward the door. "Go."

Jericho looked over at Hockley, who seemed equally conflicted, then at Garron, who said, "You heard the sheriff. Let's go."

Well, shit, when he put it like that, Jericho couldn't argue. "We'll be right next door," he told Kay on his way out, and she actually laughed.

"Lighten up, Jay—they're not going to jump me."

Jericho didn't have a response for that, so he followed Garron out of the room and stalked into his own office. Montgomery and Hockley followed him, and so, surprisingly, did Garron.

"That little punk wants her job," the old cop growled. "He's trying for a recall election so he can run against her, and he's got plenty of ammunition to shoot at her during the campaign."

Jericho shook his head. He was pretty tired for the start of the day, and it wasn't only because he'd gotten limited sleep the night before. "Does he have enough support, do you think? Can he pull it off?"

"It'll be close, I'd say. There's always been some people who have a problem with a woman in the job, and some people who don't like the idea of a dynasty or whatever. And some who'll vote for a recall because it'll add a little excitement to things, give 'em something to talk about at the hardware store. The ones causing trouble only need ten percent of the electorate to get the recall, as long as they get the wording right."

"Just a recall, though. That wouldn't be enough to kick her out?" Jericho probably should have paid a bit more attention to all this, but it had never been an issue with the LAPD and he hadn't thought it would ever be an issue in Mosely, either.

"Just an election. But Jackson will run against her and that little shit-sack has been campaigning since his first day on the job. She's busy taking care of business while he's spending all his time out kissing babies and badmouthing her to anyone who'd listen." Garron's expression was as dark as it had been back in Jericho's border-skipping days. "And how many people are going to turn out for a special election in the middle of tourist season? Maybe just Jackson's pals."

"Shit," Jericho said. Not exactly profound, but from the expressions on the others' faces, maybe not completely inappropriate.

"It's her show, though," Garron said, the warning clear in his tone. "She'll have a plan, and it'll be a hell of a lot better than whatever half-assed bullshit you come up with, so you need to do as you're told. Absolutely no cowboy crap, not on this one."

"That's the only kind of crap I *have*."

"Then keep your crap to yourself." Garron turned to look at the DEA agents. "And there can't be any federal involvement, either. One of you piping up could do her more harm than good up here—in case you hadn't noticed, most of us don't much like outsiders telling us what to do."

"Yes, we've picked up on that," Montgomery said carefully.

Jericho blew out a huff of air. "So this is another bad situation we can't do anything about? Can't help with the militia because the FBI doesn't want us. Can't do anything for Kay because—"

"You can do anything she *tells* you to do," Garron corrected. "You were in the Marines for how long, and you never learned about the chain of command and taking an order? And even in LA, cops must have bosses, don't they?"

"But getting away from all that stuff is one of the best parts of working in Mosely! More freedom, more independence. That's what Montana's all about, isn't it?"

"You start showing freedom and independence from the sheriff right now and I'll kick your ass," Garron growled. "You are loyal and obedient until I tell you otherwise. Clear?"

"*Will* you ever tell me otherwise?"

"I wouldn't count on it." And with that Garron left.

"This is an unnecessary complication," Montgomery said. Then he frowned at Hockley. "*Another* unnecessary complication. I'll leave you to deal with the other one." With that, he followed Garron and shut the door behind him.

Jericho flopped down into his battered leather desk chair. "Seriously? There's something else?"

Hockley sounded reluctant as he said, "Remember when I told you Mike DeMonte was starting to talk to us about your father's death? Remember the 'tell Junior to look closer to home' comment?"

Jericho tried to look unconcerned. "Yeah?"

"He's said more. Enough to make us think our first assumption was inaccurate."

"Not Wade, then."

"You don't seem relieved." Hockley squinted at Jericho. "You don't seem surprised, either."

"I'm just very stoic."

Another suspicious look, then Hockley gave in. "He's hinting that it was Eli's wife. Your stepmother. Nikki Crewe."

"Nikki Crewe. Isn't that a perfect eighties hair-metal name? I can see her now, with the makeup, the spandex, beating the shit out of a drum set—"

"Would you care to focus on the immediate issues? We're about to close the deal to make DeMonte go state's witness, and one of the many pieces of information he's offering us is the identity of your father's killer. Or, more accurately, evidence that will help us *prove* the identity of your father's killer. And it really seems as if that killer is Nikki Crewe."

"I hear you. But I also heard you a few days ago when you told me it was looking like Wade was the killer, so I'm trying not to go off half-cocked on any of this."

"The intel's a lot less ambiguous this time. And it definitely fits in with the previous hint."

"What kind of proof could he have, though? I mean, you've found nothing else to tie her to the scene, have you? And this long after the fact you're not likely to find any physical evidence, especially not with her house burnt down. So—is this a real case, or just something that will distract me from more important stuff?"

"Finding out who killed your father isn't important? The possibility that your stepmother, who is currently raising two small children you share blood with, may be a cold-blooded murderer isn't of concern to you?" Hockley squinted again, then leaned closer as if trying to read the truth on Jericho's face. "You already knew, didn't you?"

Jericho shook his head, maybe a little too vigorously. "I didn't and don't *know* anything." And it would have been smart to leave it there. Instead he added, "But, yeah, I had my suspicions."

"And you said nothing about them? You'd better not be planning some vigilante revenge shit, Jericho! That's exactly the kind of cowboy crap Garron was— No. That's not what you're thinking. Not your style, especially considering your relationship with your father. So what the hell's going on?"

"I can't say," Jericho replied. "I don't like it—I'd like to talk it over with you. I truly would. But I don't want to—" Well, he didn't want to put Hockley on the right track was what he didn't want to do. He didn't want to mention domestic abuse as a possible motive for the killing, not when he'd just stumbled across the evidence of that himself. But also "—I don't want to be involved in the investigation. I mean, that's what you and Montgomery were pushing for when I first came back, wasn't it? I was supposed to stay the hell out of your important fed business. So, it took me a while, but I've come 'round to your way of thinking on all that. This will be a lot tidier if I'm not involved."

"We said all that when you were a private citizen!"

"No, I was a law enforcement officer then too. But I wasn't part of the current investigation, and I'm still not. This is your show, Hockley."

Another squint. "You're not holding a grudge for that," Hockley said slowly, clearly thinking as he spoke. "Not on something this big. You've been cooperative in the past when it's really mattered. So this isn't about you being an asshole. This is— You're protecting her. The woman who killed your father. You don't want to be part of the investigation because—because you don't want her to be punished."

Jericho sighed. "I can neither confirm nor deny your wild suppositions. And how much does the DEA care who killed Eli? If it was a drug smuggler, great; you could bust them for murder if you can't catch them smuggling, which you apparently can't. But if it's not a drug-related crime, do you care anymore?"

"Are we pretending Nikki isn't smuggling shit across the border? So if I can't catch her for that, maybe I'll catch her for murder instead."

"*If* she did it. All you've got so far is Mike DeMonte's games. And he'll say anything to get out of the mess he's in, so his credibility is pretty damn low."

"Why wouldn't you want her punished?" Hockley mused.

"I think one of your early theories was that she and I were sleeping together—remember that? So maybe, in your imaginary world, I'm protecting my quasi-incestuous lover."

"Or maybe there's another reason," Hockley said. "Jericho, you're walking a fine line, here. You can't protect her—can't turn yourself into an accessory after the fact. You know that, right?"

"I don't remember you giving me this little speech when you thought *Wade* was the killer."

Hockley frowned this time rather than squinting. "You know, I think maybe—I think maybe I genuinely trusted him to look out for you. To keep you from doing something stupid. Do you believe that? I thought he'd take the fall before letting you get dragged into anything." He seemed less reflective when he added, "But I don't believe that about Nikki. She'll let you hang for her if it comes down to it. I know that."

"I know it too; hell, she'd let me hang just for the fun of watching me swing. I'm not trying to actively protect anyone, I promise. I'm neutral. For once in my life, I'm trying to keep my nose out of something that isn't my business and could get me in trouble."

Hockley didn't look persuaded, but he let it go. "Are you going to follow the same policy with the FBI and the militia?"

"Well, I'm not convinced they're not my business. The role of the sheriff's department is to serve and protect the citizens of Mosely County. Some of those militia members qualify, and so do their neighbors and a hell of a lot of other people who could get caught up in things if this goes ballistic again. It was just luck that some innocent local didn't blunder into that mess yesterday." And if someone *had* stumbled in because Jericho had pushed Kay to be aggressive instead of going around to block off the road as they'd been directed, he probably would have had to deal with that guilt until the day he died. But he tried not to think about things like that more than he had to. "So that one's not as clear-cut."

Hockley didn't seem surprised by Jericho's conclusions. "So, do you have a plan? Something to do?"

"Standard operating procedure is to wander around and poke at people until somebody gets pissed off and tells me something. But I'm open to suggestions if you've got a different method in mind."

"I'm not sure I can be involved in this one," Hockley said reluctantly. "Like you said, you've got a role because of your job, but DEA? I'm here for the border and the smugglers. I haven't got the same excuse you do."

"I'm open to suggestions even if you can't be part of enacting them." Jericho was surprised by how true that was. Hockley was uptight, sure, and he'd been generally ineffective since he'd arrived in Mosely, but that didn't make him completely useless. Mosely was a complicated jumble, and Hockley was just one of many law enforcement types who'd had trouble untangling the mess. Besides, Jericho was stumped enough to accept help from any direction.

Hockley squinted again. "What's your goal, exactly?"

"To serve and protect the people of Mosely County." That was easy. "Probably focusing on protection right now. I want to keep people safe."

"Safe from the militia."

"Mostly, yeah. I mean—from talking to Sam Tennant, I'd say his goal is to keep the people of Mosely, especially his family, safe too. But he's thinking safe from federal tyranny, not safe from—not safe from himself." Jericho pushed his chair back from the desk. "You know what? This is just one more example of outsiders coming in and messing shit up for the locals. Those guys yesterday weren't from around here. Sam Tennant's a gun-nut redneck, but he's *our* gun-nut redneck. Everything was fine up here until the other guys came in. So—I want to keep people safe from the *outsider* militia. Unless Sam's gone completely off the rails, I expect he's one of the people I should be protecting."

"You don't think he's a willing participant? The FBI tracked the other militia members to Sam's property—it was Kay's intel that made that happen."

"Maybe it kind of blew up on him. He invited some folks up for a picnic and they took advantage of his hospitality."

"Do you actually know that, or are you guessing?"

"Guessing. I don't know shit. So maybe that'll be my next step—I need to figure out what the hell's going on out there."

"And how are you going to do that? You think you're going to compete with whatever the hell intelligence gathering the FBI has set up?"

"Nope. I'm not going to gather intelligence. I'm just going to ask people what's going on. I'll start at the hardware store, maybe swing by the diner at lunchtime." He'd probably ask Wade too, but didn't bother mentioning that.

"And what will you do with what you find out?"

"I have no idea—it'll depend on what people are saying."

"Will you keep me in the loop?"

Jericho looked Hockley in the eye. "I have no idea—it'll depend on what people are saying."

It seemed like Hockley was about to object, but then Jericho's door opened and Kayla poked her head around it.

"Hey," she said quietly.

"Shit, Kay, get in here! What'd they say?" Jericho was out of his own chair, ready to offer it to her, but she carefully closed the door behind her and went to Hockley instead, nestling in by his side. He wrapped an arm around her shoulders and kissed the top of her head. So, suspicions confirmed. It was a kind of honor that they trusted Jericho enough to be open around him.

He managed to give them about five seconds of comfort-time before demanding, "What's the situation? Are they going to try for a recall?"

Kayla grimaced. "They said they didn't want to go through the mess of a recall; they thought it would be best if I just resigned." She laid her head on Hockley's chest but aimed her gaze at Jericho as she said, "They offered to accept you as acting sheriff, and honestly, Jackson's head just about lifted off his body. He couldn't stand the idea of you stepping into the role. That little—" She paused, clearly groping for the right word.

"Shit-sack?" Jericho offered. "That's Garron's professional assessment."

"Okay, yeah. That little shit-sack is so power hungry he almost came in his pants every time they mentioned a recall and special election. He thinks he's got it sewn up."

There was something nasty about that mix of imagery, but Jericho tried to ignore it. "Do you think he's right?"

"I think it would be a dangerous distraction for us to be worrying about any of this at the moment, and I told them so. I told them we need to focus on the militia, and then the shit-sack piped up, saying I couldn't be doing much work on that since the FBI had told me my help wasn't wanted." Her expression was fierce. "The arrogant fucker says *he's* got a good relationship with them and they'll do what *he* wants, but they don't trust me because of my father."

There was enough truth to the second part to make them all quiet for a moment. "I don't believe that asshole has a good relationship with *anyone*," Jericho finally said.

"But he might be political enough to win an election, and that would be trouble. So the smart thing is to appease these guys. Without their support, he might not even be able to get enough signatures for a recall, let alone the votes to win an election."

"Appease them?" Jericho asked carefully.

"They don't want me, but they'll accept you. You're better than Jackson, Jay."

"But you're better than both of us."

"Yeah, I am. So that's why I told them I wasn't going to step down, not for you, not for anyone."

Jericho grinned at her. "Good for you."

"What did they say?" Hockley asked.

"They're going to think it over. Which probably means they've got the petitions already drawn up and they just need time to get the signatures."

"So what do we do?" Jericho had been sitting still too long; it was time for action. "Do you start campaigning now? Should we dig up some scandal on Jackson? I bet there's something—anyone that slimy will definitely have left a trail."

"No," Kay said firmly. "We just do our jobs to the best of our ability. We keep an eye on the feds—sorry, the FBI, not all feds—and make sure they aren't taking unnecessary risks with our citizens. We up our patrols, make sure we're seen in the community, make sure people aren't freaking out. We activate all our channels of communication and figure out what people are thinking, what they're noticing. And, Jay, if we find anything useful, we report it to the FBI."

He smiled blandly at her. Not agreement, but not disagreement, either. She raised an eyebrow, but didn't speak. She'd wait until the time came, and make her fight then. Nice that they understood each other.

"Okay, then," he said. "I'll go and see what people have to say." He stood up, found his keys, then turned to face Kayla and Hockley. "And if anyone asks—is the official department terminology for Jackson 'shit-sack,' or are we going with 'little fucker' instead?"

"Don't cause trouble, Jericho," Kayla warned. "And since the lab has your Glock, sign out a sidearm from Garron before you leave the building."

"That's a mixed message, isn't it?"

"Just because someone isn't *causing* trouble, it doesn't mean trouble won't find them." She frowned. "Especially in your case. So if you're in uniform, you're armed. Clear?"

"Yes, ma'am," he said obediently as he shut the door. Strange to leave the two of them in his office, but they could probably use a hideout.

He headed off to find Garron, then out into the town. Not looking for trouble, no. But he sure wouldn't mind if some of it found him.

CHAPTER 3

Jericho heard about a hundred variations on "this doesn't seem like something Sam Tennant's boys would do" over the next few hours, and he couldn't disagree with a single one. Well, he wasn't willing to go as far as Mrs. Spooner at the post office, who said Sam was too gentle to even swat a fly, but the rest of the town seemed more realistic. Sam talked tough, but he wasn't the sort to declare war.

The town also seemed genuinely concerned over the rhetoric flaring up on the internet. The news channels had sent crews, and when Jericho arrived, Lincoln at the motel was scrambling; it was tourist season *and* most of his rooms were already full of feds, so he was calling neighboring towns, the closest a good half-hour drive, and seeing what they could offer. Knowing Lincoln, he was expecting some sort of finder's fee for his services.

"How long you planning to stay for?" Jericho asked a man in an MSNBC jacket as the news crews waited for Lincoln to give them instructions.

"Not sure," the man replied. "We've already got enough footage of the scene from yesterday; we didn't get here in time for anything but the cleanup, though. We covered the FBI news conference this morning, but they weren't saying too much. Right now, we're supposed to wait a few days and see if anything happens. If people start coming in from out of state like they're saying on the internet, there could be quite a show."

A show, Jericho mused as he headed back to his cruiser. A backwater town that had already dealt with a police corruption scandal, the potential of a biker war, and a serial killer, and now it was facing out-of-state militia violence, and the media thought it would be *a show.*

He checked in at the hardware store and found Mr. Appleby at the center of a crowd of concerned citizens. Most of them were older men, born and raised in Mosely. They'd probably known Sam Tennant since his BB gun days. Jericho took off his hat and nodded respectfully, and a few of the men nodded back.

"Will's taking some time off," Mr. Appleby said. He made it sound like a casual thing, but how could it be? Will had been traumatized by his mistaken arrest, his time in jail and by the violence he'd witnessed before he got there—none of that pain would be resolved by a little vacation.

And Jericho had been responsible for at least some of it. But there was no point in talking about things that couldn't be changed, so he just said, "Let me know if I can be any help with that."

"What about Sam Tennant and his boys?" one of the other men demanded.

Jericho turned to look at him. "Mr. Pauls?" It was a guess, but with a nose that blended into his forehead like that, a pretty safe one. The Pauls were well-known for their particular brand of ugly. And the man's glare softened a little, so Jericho figured he'd gotten it right. It never hurt to remind people that Jericho knew them, knew their families and their ways of life. He might have been away for a while, but he wasn't a stranger. "I'm hoping to hear from you all about Sam," he said, addressing most of the crowd. "I'm trying to understand what the hell went wrong yesterday, and what we can do to fix it without anyone else getting hurt."

"None of that yesterday was Sam's fault," Mr. Pauls said, his jaw jutting out like he was still ready for a fight. "It's all these outsiders, flying in from Washington DC or wherever and thinking they can tell us how to live our lives!"

The group fell silent, staring at Jericho expectantly. They wanted to see where his loyalties were, and his answer would probably determine the level of cooperation he could expect not only from them but from their networks of family and friends. In a small town, every damn word sent ripples out into the community.

So he kept his body relaxed and friendly as he said, "I'm wondering if you're right about the outsiders. Not the feds, maybe—I was on-site yesterday, and the way that was laid out? The feds got ambushed, for sure. If they'd been looking to start something they would have been a hell of a lot better armed, and there would have been a larger team. But it wasn't Sam or his boys doing the ambushing. We've got names for most of the guys who got arrested or killed, and they're not locals. But what I'm trying to figure out is what the hell they were doing here." *And are more of them likely to show up?* "You guys heard anything about any of that?"

He scanned the crowd. "Boxie, you still delivering propane? They got a furnace out at Sam's, or they just burning wood?"

There was a pause as the man decided whether to answer. Or just a pause because this was Boxie Bocksteader, and he didn't do, think, or say anything quickly. Finally he rumbled, "Wood furnace. Big old one in the back of the main house. Takes six-foot logs."

That was more than Jericho needed to know about the home heating choices of the Tennant clan, but it was interesting that Boxie knew it. "You spent much time out there lately? Helping them get wood in for the winter?"

"So what if he has?" Mr. Pauls demanded. "Is that a crime, now?"

Possibly this interview would have gone better if Jericho had gotten Boxie alone before starting, but really, he wasn't asking questions in order to get specific information so much as he was playing a role, making sure that everyone in the store knew he was benign and interested and willing to listen. It was about the same thing he'd done every other place he'd visited, only with a slightly more hostile audience this time.

Or *some* of the audience was hostile. But Mr. Appleby stepped easily out from behind the counter and said, "Settle down, Pauly. Jericho isn't the problem here."

"Neither's Sam Tennant."

"So if he isn't the problem, then he's *got* a problem," Jericho said firmly. "The feds are looking in his direction, and they lost men yesterday, so they're looking *hard*. For what it's worth, I agree with you all—this doesn't sound like Sam Tennant. But he's mixed up in it somehow. My main goal is just trying to find a way to get him out of it, and to keep any other locals from getting dragged in."

"Those are pretty words," Mr. Pauls sneered.

"Well, that makes sense, since I'm such a pretty man," Jericho answered. Mr. Pauls's expression didn't mellow, but at least he shut up, and Jericho turned his attention to the others. "I've got no reason to try to hurt Sam, and plenty of reasons to try to help him. So if anyone has anything useful, any ideas about what's going on, I'd like to hear them." He waited a moment, long enough to give people a chance to speak up but not long enough so it'd seem like he'd been denied. "You all know where to find me. And I'd appreciate it if you'd spread the word; the more information we have, the better the chance we can get things tidied up without more trouble."

"We?" one of the men asked.

"The sheriff's department." Maybe the department would share the information with the feds, maybe they wouldn't.

Other than Mr. Pauls, the men seemed generally cooperative after that, but they didn't have any new leads. *Nobody* seemed to know much past the basics, Jericho reflected as he drove back through town. Sam's group had been puttering along at low-grade nuisance level for years, then had suddenly flared up to suicidal intensity, and nobody in town had any idea why. Jericho had killed three men the day before, and *he* had no damn idea why.

He should go back to the station. The FBI would have finished their preliminary interrogations of the survivors from the day before, and maybe there'd be some useful information floating around there. Sure, it would take a bit of digging to get at it since the feds weren't being cooperative, but it wasn't like Jericho was being useful out in the community.

Yeah, it would make sense to go back to the station. That was what Jericho was thinking, even as he drove up to Scotty Hawk's garage, found a parking spot, and locked the car. He'd do the smart thing—soon.

But first, he'd do a little more poking.

Scotty had a pickup on the hoist and was leaning against the wall watching oil drain out of the engine. He scowled when Jericho walked in. "You're bad for business, Crewe."

"The bikers, you mean?" It wasn't a huge stretch—quite a few of the recently arrested men had been Scotty's customers or employees. "I can't take the credit or the blame; it was the feds who busted them."

"And we both know why the feds did that," Scotty retorted. He took a quick look around to make sure no one was in earshot, then said, "Wade might not have set them up if you hadn't started poking around."

"Wade was the one who *started* me poking around." Jericho was oddly insulted by all this. "If anyone's bad for business, it's *Wade*."

"But he brings in other business. You don't bring anything but trouble."

"I rented a truck from you, and you totally gouged me on the price. Don't I get any credit for that?"

"That credit's used up. What do you want?"

Well, Jericho had been hoping Wade might have been at the garage, but he wouldn't admit to that. "I'm touring around today, checking in on people about the situation out at Sam Tennant's. I'm trying to figure out why it all exploded like it did, and trying to make sure it doesn't blow up again. Sam brings his trucks in to you, doesn't he?" It was a pretty safe guess, since Scotty was the only mechanic in town.

"They do most of their work themselves—part of their survivalist bullshit. But, yeah, he's bought parts from me a few times. So what?"

"Just wondering when you'd seen him last. Wondering if he'd said anything unusual or . . .?"

"This is seriously how you're spending your day? You're driving around, asking people about the last time they talked to Sam Tennant?"

"Yeah. It's how I'm spending my day. So what can you tell me about the last time you talked to Sam Tennant?"

"I think he mentioned something about planning a big ambush against federal agents. Yeah, that's right, that's what he said. He said he was sick of fucking cops coming by and asking stupid fucking questions, and the next fucking cop who did it was going to get the shit kicked out of him. That's what he said."

And with that, Jericho's patience was gone. He forced a smile, then stepped in closer. "So what's your plan, Scotty? You don't want me involved, don't want me asking questions—you just want to sit back and watch the feds and the damn militia get in a war on Main Street? Is that how you think this should get solved?"

Scotty didn't step back or look away. "If the feds get the fuck out of town, there won't be a war. If they mind their own business, this can all just stop."

"It's a bit late for that. There's two dead feds now, and the rest aren't going to just walk away from that. Even if they wanted to, they couldn't—every asshole in the country would be gunning for them from now on if there's no reprisal for this."

"Not my problem," Scotty said. "And it's *three* dead feds. The chick died—it was on the news."

There was something about the way he said it, a trace of smug satisfaction that made Jericho's fists clench. "She died for doing her job, and you think it's no big deal. It's not your problem."

"She was doing the wrong job." Scotty's smirk made it clear he knew he was getting to Jericho. "She should have kept her fat ass at home in the kitchen, and she would have been fine."

Jericho nodded, his neck muscles so tight they were almost shaking. *Every* muscle so tight they were almost shaking. He took a step back and nodded again, forcing himself to relax.

"Thanks for your help today, Scotty." He kept his voice quiet and level. "I'll absolutely remember it when I have the chance to pay you back."

The big mechanic squinted at him. "You sounded like your dad for a second there," he said, and for the first time there was a trace of doubt in his voice.

"Yeah?" Jericho smiled, and knew exactly what Scotty was talking about, because he could almost *feel* his father's expression on his own face, the way his lips lifted to show his canines as his eyes stayed cold. "I guess blood comes through in the end."

"Don't go getting all bent out of shape," Scotty said quickly. "I was just talking, just pulling your chain."

"Sure." Jericho still felt it, his father's cold menace. And he didn't care if Scotty was feeling it too. "Nothing to worry about, Scotty. Nothing to lose any sleep over." And as he took another step backward, he sent his gaze around the service bay, taking in the tidily arranged tools and the haphazard pile of trash in the corner. "You ever worry about fire in here? All the oil, and the rags? This place would go up easy if it ever caught a spark, wouldn't it?"

"Jesus Christ, I was just *talking*!"

"Of course you were." Some part of Jericho was screaming at him, appalled at seeing him become the sort of bully he'd always despised. But another part was purring in satisfaction. "And the next time we talk, you'll either have something useful to say or you'll keep your mouth shut. Right, Scotty?"

"Yeah, fine." Scotty puffed his chest up like he was trying to pull his courage back together, maybe getting ready for another round, but Jericho was done with it. He turned and left without another word.

It would have been almost reassuring to tell himself he'd been channeling Wade with that little show, but he knew better. Wade was dangerous, but in a sly, slippery way. He wouldn't make threats, not even veiled threats; he'd just make a plan, and then carry it out without warning.

Intimidation? No, that wasn't coming from Wade. It was coming from Eli. Or, worse to consider, maybe there was no one else to blame. Maybe that had been pure Jericho.

CHAPTER 4

"They're not telling us anything," Kayla said, throwing a disgusted glare in the direction of the sheriff's department conference room. The FBI base was in there, and the door to the outer office was carefully closed. "But they don't need to, not with the damn reporters and the internet."

Jericho nodded, scanning the computer screen in front of him. They were in Kayla's office, but she'd given up her desk chair so he could get a better view. Hockley and Montgomery were standing on the other side of the desk, watching him read. "They're actually doing it," he said. "These militia psychos are trying to make Mosely the site for their big showdown?"

"They're being a bit vague," Hockley said. "Mostly saying Northwestern Montana. But they're using yesterday's incident—all facts totally distorted, of course—as their excuse, so it's clear what they're talking about."

"Shit." Jericho leaned back in the chair and looked at Kayla. "I didn't get anything useful from anyone in town. But that makes sense if this is an out-of-state effort."

"Nothing about this 'makes sense' in any way I'd want to use the phrase." She frowned at him, then at the other two. "But I have to make decisions based on the information we've got. And what we've got says these assholes are getting bolder. Nevada, then Oregon, then yesterday's shit show—it might not be all the same groups, but it's the same movement. And they're escalating."

"The FBI is ramping up their response," Montgomery said, sounding almost defensive. "We may not have details, but we know they're shipping in SWAT teams and extra agents. They're taking this seriously."

"But whatever they do to take the militia down could get messy." Kayla shoved Jericho's shoulder to prod him out of her chair. "And the mess could hurt our citizens." She sank into the vacated seat and started clicking the mouse. "If half of what this Lucas Templeton asshole says is true, the out-of-staters are coming in heavily armed and *hungry* for a fight. He's got them worked up into thinking this is the beginning of the end. They're going to start a revolution, right here in Mosely."

"When people talk about border towns being rough, I think they usually mean the *other* border," Jericho said, partly to himself. "There shouldn't be this much going on in Mosely, Montana."

"I'll just send an email to Templeton and let him know that," Kay said sarcastically. "I'm sure he'll see the problem and go on back home."

"Or down to Texas or wherever." Jericho shrugged. "Doesn't have to be home. Just shouldn't be here."

"Meanwhile, back in reality," Montgomery broke in, "we're going to do the smart thing, right? We're going to let the FBI handle this without poking our noses in where they don't belong?"

Kayla looked at Jericho, then shrugged. "At the moment? Since we don't have any ideas for anything constructive to do? Sure, yeah, we'll keep out of it."

Montgomery clearly wasn't satisfied with that answer, but it wasn't Kayla's job to satisfy him and he seemed to realize it. He and Jericho left her office together but separated as soon as they were out the door, Montgomery off to do whatever the hell he did when he wasn't getting in Jericho's way, and Jericho heading to his office to read more internet bullshit. There were no names given in the media descriptions of the shoot-outs, luckily, and the law enforcement side was generally described as FBI with local support. Nothing to point unwanted attention toward him.

He needed to regain his apathy from the day before. Needed to remember that he didn't like his job very much and was trying to escape from it. If he took a paycheck for a little longer and just sat around the office pushing paper, that was fine. Why was he getting all worked up about not being involved in something he didn't *want* to be involved in?

And of course Wade had predicted this, the smug bastard. *"If you want me to believe you really don't care about your job, then you need to keep not caring about it for a period of time."* Jericho had managed to not care for about three days, and for two of them he'd been out of town. Damn it.

He did some paperwork, enough to remind himself that the job *was* pretty annoying, and when his cell rang he reached for it like a life preserver. Seeing the unfamiliar number on the display made the call even more interesting; Wade had a tendency to call from strange places or burner phones, and talking to Wade would make the whole day a hell of a lot better.

"Crewe," he said into the mouthpiece, and sure enough, it was Wade's familiar voice that replied.

"Come meet me. You know where."

"Yeah?" Jericho checked the wall clock. It was almost six, and it wasn't like he was doing anything important. He could leave, guilt-free. But why should he drive all the way up into the mountains to meet Wade at a dingy old cabin when they could be at the apartment instead?

He had his mouth open to comment on that when Wade added, "Bring Kay."

Jericho's imagination slammed to a halt. Kayla. Wade wasn't—no. He wasn't suggesting that. This was something else entirely, and the remote setting suddenly made sense.

"Okay," Jericho agreed. "See you soon."

Kayla raised her eyebrows in question when he stuck his head into her office and invited her to join him for dinner, but she didn't protest, just grabbed her jacket and hat, strapped on her borrowed sidearm, and followed him out the door. They were halfway to the car when she said, "I actually *am* hungry."

"Wade wants a meeting," Jericho said. "Food wasn't mentioned."

"Strange world," she mused as she cut in front of Jericho and headed for the driver's seat of her cruiser. "A known criminal wants a meeting, so the sheriff doesn't get dinner."

"We could hit the drive-through," Jericho offered, "except Mosely doesn't have one."

"Where's the meeting?"

"Up by the old copper mine." It occurred to Jericho that he and Kay had visited the cabin together a few times in high school when he'd been experimenting with heterosexuality. Possibly it would be a bit awkward to go back there with her. And possibly Wade had already thought of this complication, the bastard. "That cabin," he said, and left it alone.

She glanced over at him. "Wade asked you to bring me to a meeting at the cabin by the copper mine?"

Jericho kept his gaze fixed out the front windshield. "Yup."

"Did he mention a reason?"

"Nope."

"But you think it's important."

"You're not his favorite person, Kay. He's probably not just looking for a chance to catch up on old times."

She was silent for a while, then said, "Even before you came back? Before you and Wade started whatever you and Wade have started? Or restarted, I guess. Even back then, if Wade had called me and asked me to meet him in a remote location, I would have gone." She sounded thoughtful. "I know he's a criminal. A *dangerous* criminal. I might not have enough evidence to get any convictions, but that doesn't change what I know. And still, I would have met with him, and I wouldn't have been worried about my safety. Like I'd have thought he wouldn't hurt me for old times' sake."

Jericho wasn't sure what to say, so he waited, and eventually she said, "I can't figure out if that means there's something trustworthy about him, or if I'm hopelessly naïve."

"When dealing with Wade, I've found it's best to generally avoid any black-and-white answers." Jericho smiled despite himself. "It's entirely possible there's something trustworthy about him *and* you're hopelessly naïve. Just like it's possible you're not his favorite person *and* he wouldn't hurt you because of old times."

"And you don't find that kind of . . . hard to manage?"

Jericho shrugged, almost shy. "I guess I think it's worth it."

Kayla didn't respond to that, and they drove the rest of the way up into the mountains in silence.

When they arrived at the cabin, an unfamiliar truck was parked on the rutted track, and two men stepped away from the bumper. It was almost full dark, but Jericho recognized Wade easily. The other—

"Shit," Kayla said. "That's Sam Tennant."

"It appears the feds don't have the compound quite as contained as they think." Jericho tried not to be smug, but didn't try all that hard.

Kayla sighed and turned the engine off, then pushed her door open, and Jericho climbed out with her.

"Heard you were asking about me," Sam Tennant said, his gaze on Jericho, sounding belligerent. "Heard you think you need to *save* me."

"Nah," Jericho drawled. He stepped closer to the other two and said, "If you invited this shit into our town, I don't have any interest in saving you or helping you out. I was trying to be sure you *did* invite it. Because if you didn't? Then, yeah, in that case I'd assume you'd be hoping for some help."

"And you think I'd want it from you?"

Jericho turned to Wade. "So, we're here for a friendly visit? Good to see you, of course, but maybe next time we could stay in town."

Wade smiled and turned to Sam. "Would you rather just talk to the sheriff? Jay can be a bit annoying sometimes."

Sam huffed, then turned to Kayla. "I've got family at the ranch. I'm going back out to them, and I'm going to do whatever it takes to keep them safe. My grandkids are out there—two of them in diapers. They're just little kids. You understand that?"

"I do," she said calmly. "What do you think is the chief threat to their safety at the current time?"

"Goddamn motherfucking feds!" His voice rang through the surrounding forest.

"So why the ambush?" Kayla asked. "I agree, the feds are a serious issue. I think they'll absolutely try to keep the kids safe—even if you don't believe they'll do it out of goodness, they'll want to avoid the bad press. But the ambush? Three dead agents? You had to know that would heat things up."

Tennant didn't reply immediately, so Jericho added, "If this had been an act of war on your part—if you were genuinely planning to take on the federal government, for whatever deluded reasons—you'd have evacuated the kids first. You're not stupid, Sam. So why didn't you do that?"

Sam grimaced at him, then turned back to Kayla. "That's not what we need to talk about. We need to talk about getting the kids off the ranch *now*, not a couple days ago. I had to sneak out with a herd of cattle so the fucking feds wouldn't catch me on their damn infrared or whatever, then hike through the woods to the border, then—" He stopped as if realizing it might not be a good idea to share too many details of his daring escape. "Kids couldn't do it, is what I'm saying. And—" He looked at the ground, then over at Wade, then spat a nasty glob that landed too close to Jericho's boot. "My guests want the kids to stay."

"As human shields?" Jericho demanded. Why else would hard-core militants want a bunch of kids around? "They're using your kin like that, and you're still calling them your *guests*?"

"I'm sure it's a complicated situation," Kayla said, throwing a quick glare in Jericho's direction before smiling sympathetically at Tennant. "But we're all on the same page, here. The children's safety is the most important priority. So we need to work together to take care of that."

"You got any bright ideas?" Tennant asked cynically.

"I don't have as much background information as I need, Sam, and you know that. So if you have a plan, I'd like to hear it, but otherwise, you need to tell me a bit more about what the hell's going on and who we're dealing with." Kayla glanced in Jericho's direction, then added, "And maybe it'd be best if this was a smaller conversation. Jay, Wade, can you two take a walk and keep an eye on the road, make sure we're not going to be disturbed?"

It wasn't a dismissal, and Jericho knew it. Kay was giving him a chance to talk to Wade alone in order to get information out of him. It was a good strategy, but it sucked to have to take Sam Tennant's smirk.

Wade probably knew what Kayla was up to, since he always knew what everybody was up to, and he cooperated, following Jericho down the rough dirt road without comment. When they were far enough away that soft voices wouldn't be heard, but still close enough to get back to Kayla if she called out, Wade said, "He met them on the internet. You believe that shit? Like, internet dating, but without any sex, and for militia assholes."

"And this was their first in-person meeting?"

"Nah. Sam went down and met up with some of them in Nevada, he says. Says they seemed like okay guys—big talkers, he figured, but most of these assholes are. I don't think he had any idea they were going to take it this far."

"And how far are they taking it? What's the damn plan, here?"

"They honestly think they're going to start a war." Wade sounded amazed, maybe even impressed by the level of delusion. "They think there are militias all over the country who've just been waiting for an excuse like this, and they think those whack jobs are all going to come up here and join in, or else rise up in their own locations. They think this is the start of the revolution."

Jericho squinted at him. "You get that all from Sam?"

Wade grimaced. "Well, maybe that's something we should talk about."

"Jesus, Wade! Tell me you're not involved with these people!"

"Not directly," Wade said quickly. He was watching Jericho, obviously waiting for the reaction. When Jericho gave him none, he sighed and continued. "Not philosophically, at all. I mean, the feds are a pain in the ass, but I'd rather work around them than take them on head-to-head. I'm not suicidal."

"But . . ." Jericho prompted. He wasn't sure he wanted to hear the rest.

Wade shrugged. "But they sometimes need things taken across the border, and, well, that's my specialty. So I've spent time out at Sam's place. Over the last couple weeks, I've heard rumblings. And then, yeah, he told me more tonight."

"And you didn't bother to mention any of this to me."

"Is there some part of you being a cop and me being a robber that you don't understand, Jay? Of course I didn't mention that I'd been gunrunning for a seditious militia."

"There are dead feds," Jericho hissed. He wasn't sure why it seemed important to keep those words quiet; everyone in the state knew about the dead feds. "This is a fucking huge case, Wade, and the FBI is all the hell over it! They're going to be digging into every damn nook and cranny, and they're *definitely* going to want to know where the damn guns came from!"

"I'm aware of that. And if I'd known these fuckers were going to be as crazy as they've turned out to be, I wouldn't have gotten involved." Wade frowned at the ground, then shrugged. "I *probably* wouldn't have gotten involved. But by the time I understood how serious they were, it was too late."

It sounded like Wade was actually admitting to a mistake, and a part of Jericho wanted to take a moment to celebrate the unheard of occurrence. But he didn't have time for gloating. "Give me names. Give me every detail you can, tell me everything that might ever be important about this, and maybe we can cut a deal. The DEA will be pissed, but the FBI doesn't care about you, not anymore. You haven't gunned down any feds."

"Well, there was that one."

"He was crooked. It doesn't count when they're crooked."

Wade nodded his understanding, but Jericho knew that was all the gesture meant. Wade understood, but he wasn't agreeing to anything. And sure enough, after a moment he said, "You know I can't do that, Jay. I can't make a deal."

"Can't? No, that's not the word you should use. You should just say you *won't* do it. That'd be a hell of a lot more honest."

Wade's smile was gentle. "What do you think would happen to me if I made a deal with the feds?" He waited for half a second, not long enough for Jericho to process the emotions the question had caused, then leaned in closer. "What do you think happened to Mike DeMonte this afternoon? He talked, and—"

"Wait. What? Mike DeMonte? What the hell happened to him?"

Wade seemed genuinely surprised. "You hadn't heard about that yet?"

"Heard about *what*?"

"Mike's dead, Jay. The wrong people heard he was talking, and they shut him up. Seriously, nobody thought to mention that to you?"

"Jesus Christ." Jericho's stomach churned, and he half turned to face the forest, searching for some calm. He hadn't liked Mike; the guy had been a damn psychopath. But still. "He was in protective custody. How the hell did they get to him?"

"The protective custody slowed them down, but it didn't stop them. Nothing will stop them." Wade shuffled around so he was in front of Jericho again. "So when I say I can't make a deal? I mean I don't want to, sure. I don't want to break the code, don't want to betray people who've trusted me. But I also mean I *can't*, not if I want to stay alive. And I *do* want to stay alive." He grinned like a little boy. "Especially now that you're back. You've stirred shit up, and I definitely want to be around to see what the world looks like when it's all settled."

"If I understand your imagery, the world's going to be covered in a layer of shit."

"The world's *always* covered in a layer of shit. But sometimes it's thicker in certain areas, thinner in others."

Jericho stared at Wade's shoes and tried to organize his thoughts. He couldn't let himself be led into the shifting sands of Wade's conversation; this was no time to talk about the world, or how shit-covered it was. "Mike DeMonte is dead." He glanced up. "That's handy for you. And for Nikki. He was about the only witness tying her to Eli's death, and I don't even want to know how much he had on you."

Wade shrugged. "It's handy for ex-Sheriff Morgan too—it shut up one of the witnesses against him and probably put a pretty good scare into the others. And I wasn't disappointed to hear the news, no. But there were other parties—much more powerful parties—that had at least as many reasons to want him shut up. He did some deals with the militia, and the Chicago crew didn't just disappear. It could have been a lot of people, Jay."

He hadn't firmly denied his own involvement, but Jericho didn't have the heart to push for any more. Instead he said, "So what else is going on with the militia? What can you give me?"

Wade sighed. "I can't give you much you don't already have or can't guess for yourself. The only names I know, you've already got. I'm not sure about numbers. The last time I was out there it was just Sam's crew—maybe thirty people in his family and their gang, maybe fifteen or twenty of them active in the militia part of things—plus a couple of these new guys. Rumor is the number's a hell of a lot bigger now, but I don't know if that's true, and Sam wouldn't tell me."

"So if you haven't been out there, how'd you hook up with Sam tonight?"

"He wanted to talk to you, so he contacted Scotty and Scotty passed the message on." Wade raised his eyebrows. "Guess it's not only the feds keeping track of things between you and me."

"Really? What the hell happened between Sam wanting to talk to me and him coming on so strong a few minutes ago?"

"He's putting on a show. Pride, you know? He's a big talker with his militia bullshit about personal responsibility and laying down your life for your beliefs, but now that it's actually happening, he's running scared. Kay can handle him better than you would—she's got a bit of tact, now and then."

"So what's he not going to tell her? What can you tell me that she isn't going to hear?"

"Not much." Wade didn't seem too worried about his lack of helpful hints. "Except maybe that these guys—they're deluded, no doubt. But they're not stupid. That mess yesterday? They wanted that. I don't have confirmation, but I believe it was one of them who called the tip in to Kay about the arms shipment. They *wanted* her to bring in the feds, wanted things to go to shit just like they have. And once things got started yesterday? I don't know the details of how they saw it playing out, but they had to know reinforcements were on the way and they could have escaped. Taken the two kills and fought another day. That would have been the smart move, but they didn't take it; I don't know why, but it wasn't because they were too stupid to know what was going to happen to them. You know?"

"Trying to become martyrs," Jericho said. It wasn't exactly a new idea.

"Yeah," Wade agreed, "but living martyrs really aren't that impressive. Those boys took themselves out of the fight for the rest of their lives, and for what? They can say some crazy shit at the trial, get some coverage they wouldn't have gotten if they'd been dead. But I don't know if that's enough for them." He shrugged. "It sure as hell wouldn't be enough for me."

"So what are they up to, then? What's the next step?"

"I have no idea." Wade shook his head. "And I don't think Sam knows, either. They've practically got him held hostage—he had to get their permission to leave tonight—one of his grandkids is diabetic and was low on insulin, so they let him sneak to town to go get more. Everything under their control, they've got totally planned out, but a sick kid? That's something they couldn't have foreseen."

"But Sam could have. If he'd known the showdown was going to happen, he could have gotten the kids out of there, or at least stocked up on medicine."

"Yeah. And hopefully that's what he's telling Kay."

"So—damn. What are we supposed to do with any of this information? Sit back and wait for their next move?"

"How about we do our sitting back on a beach somewhere?" Wade suggested. "You were only sticking around to help Kay out with this, but the feds have taken over now. So you're right, you don't have a role to play. Let's get the hell out of town, you and me."

"I can't do that."

Wade smiled as if it was the answer he'd expected. "If you keep saying shit like that, I don't want to hear any more lectures from you about the difference between *can't* and *won't*."

That was probably fair. "You really think it's going to be that bad? Like, leaving-town bad?"

"Yeah," Wade said slowly. He looked reflective. "I don't know these guys too well, but I know you; you like to be in the middle of shit. And this isn't something you should be in the middle of. Whatever happens, it's going to be ugly."

Jericho didn't respond, and Wade snorted. "And that just made you determined to be in the middle of it, right? I swear, Jay, you've got more balls than brains."

"I killed three men yesterday." It had been popping into his mind uninvited all day, the cold reality of it. "I don't know why it happened, but it did. I can't— Shit, I *won't* walk away and pretend I'm not involved. And I have a responsibility to the town, and to Kay—"

"How many men have you killed in your life, Jay? I mean—how many tours of Afghanistan did you do? And you were out in the field, not pushing paper somewhere. Don't tell me you only started killing people since you got back to Mosely."

There was a throbbing in Jericho's head: not quite pain, just an awareness of pressure. He wished it would go the hell away. "I've killed a lot of people," he admitted. "And, I don't know, maybe I'm being racist, thinking these people matter more because they're in the US— but we were at *war* in Afghanistan. We're not at war here."

"I think the militia gang would disagree with you on that."

The two of them stood in silence for a while, and then Kayla called, "Jay? Ready to go?"

"Yeah," he called back, then, in a quieter voice, asked Wade, "You going to come by later? Or we could— Shit, I don't even know where you live. You want to meet at your place?"

"Can't." Wade didn't sound too broken up about it. "I've got work to do."

"With everything that's going on? Shit, Wade, that's not smart! There are feds everywhere."

"That's part of the fun," Wade replied with a jaunty smile, and he started back toward the others.

CHAPTER 5

Of course Kayla insisted on taking all the information to the FBI, and of course they downplayed the value of her intel while playing up her decision not to arrest Sam Tennant and bring him in so *they* could question him.

"It would have cut off a potential stream of information," Kayla said. She and Jericho were behind her desk with a room full of senior agents frowning at them. "We would have blown the trust not just from Tennant, but Granger as well. As it is, they're working with us, trying to de-escalate the situation. If I'd brought Tennant in, he wouldn't have been able to feed us any more information *and* it might have endangered the child at the compound."

"Or we could have used the insulin as a bargaining chip for some other concession," Special Agent Casey said. He seemed to have aged about ten years since the morning, and he'd already looked pretty shitty back then.

But him having a hard time was no excuse for sloppy thinking, so Jericho said, "You're assuming anyone in charge out there gives a shit about the kid. I don't think that's a safe assumption. Hell, if the martyrdom theory is accurate and this is all about publicity and perception, they'd love it if they ended up with a dead kid they could blame on the big, bad feds. You think they wouldn't have an internet field day with you even mentioning the possibility of withholding a kid's medicine?"

Casey scowled at him. "Why were you contacted in the first place? And why didn't you inform me of the meeting *before* it occurred?"

"I was contacted because I'm a local—they know me, and they know the sheriff. Come on, Casey, this isn't news to you. When the feds roll into town they're supposed to work with the locals because we're the ones who know the players. You lost some people, and it's made you want to be a cowboy—believe me, I understand the cowboy instinct—but that doesn't mean it's good police work. You should be using us, not ignoring us." He waited a moment, saw no sign of softening in Casey's glare, and added, "And I didn't tell you about the meeting before we went out because I didn't know what it was about. It could have been anything, any of the large number of concerns we deal with in this county. I didn't know it was militia until we got there and saw Sam." He managed to keep himself from saying that if he had known, he still wouldn't have told the feds. Hopefully Kayla would appreciate his discretion.

"You're aware of the penalties for impeding a federal investigation?" Casey demanded.

"Is that the best way to spend your energy?" Kayla asked. Her voice was gentle, but surely Casey wouldn't be stupid enough to miss the strength behind her words. "I understand that you're frustrated; I can't imagine having to *negotiate* with the assholes responsible for the death of any of my deputies. But we're on the same side here. We're not trying to get in your way; we were simply responding to a call."

"And we're all just pretending you got that call because you're *locals*," Casey said. "We're supposed to ignore the relationship between your under-sheriff and one of the suspects in this investigation?"

"I was unaware that Mr. Granger was a suspect in this case," Kayla said, still calm. "As you know—as you *ordered*—my department hasn't been made privy to your investigations. In terms of other cases?" She shrugged. "Again, I don't think worrying about my other cases is the best place for you to spend your energy. Do you?"

Casey clearly wasn't interested in Kay's advice about where to direct his efforts, but her points were pretty hard for anyone to argue with. Instead he growled, "I'm watching both of you," and then stalked away.

"Aren't you glad you talked to them?" Jericho asked as the other FBI agents trailed after their boss.

"Yes, I *am* glad," Kayla said. "Because I know I did my job. I did what I should do, and I didn't let someone else's issues interfere."

Well she was more mature than Jericho, but that was hardly news. He watched the feds leave, then said, "Shit. We're back where we started, right? We still don't have anything to work on."

"We have the 'large number of concerns we deal with in this county.' Don't think they've gone anywhere."

"You want me to go check on Mr. Williton's traps again, make sure he's not catching the neighbors' cats?"

Kayla looked at the clock on the wall and shook her head. "No. I think a fourteen-hour day is enough. I want you to go home and get some sleep, and come back bright-eyed and bushy-tailed tomorrow."

"And you're going to do the same?" he prompted. "I've heard that voters like a sheriff with a nice bushy tail."

"Good tip," Kayla said, starting to pack up her gear, clearly ready for the conversation to end.

Maybe a little too ready. "Have you heard anything else about that?" Jericho asked. "Has the shit-sack done anything new?"

"He's the least of my worries," Kayla said. Maybe she even meant it. "That situation will either take care of itself or it won't, but I'm not going to waste any more energy on it."

Jericho would have liked to argue with that; taking steps to preserve a job Kayla loved shouldn't be classified as wasting energy. But she didn't seem too receptive to his ideas right then, so he saved them.

Instead he went home to his beige apartment, tried not to notice how empty it felt, and pretended he was simply unwinding as he sat on the couch and sipped a beer, watching TV. He wasn't waiting for Wade, of course. He wasn't that desperate.

When he finally found his way to bed, he slept on the side Wade had occupied the night before, but only for variety, not because he was hoping to smell Wade on the pillow or the sheets. And when his phone rang at three in the morning, he answered it before the second ring because he was a man of action, not because he'd been lying there unable to sleep.

"The question you should be asking yourself," Wade said in response to Jericho's greeting, "isn't how many men you've killed. The question you should be asking is how many *innocent* men you've killed. When you were at war, they were trying to kill you. And since you got home—how many men have you killed who weren't part of something dirty?"

Was that the better question? Jericho certainly didn't have to think very hard to answer it. "None. I've never killed an innocent person."

"Me neither," Wade said quietly.

Jericho hadn't realized he'd needed the words until they'd been spoken. But once he heard them he felt lighter, as if the world was a better place than it had been moments before.

"Okay," he said. "That's good to know."

"I've done other bad things to innocent people," Wade said quickly. "And I lie to them all the time, sometimes without even having a good reason. Innocent people do *not* like me, in general. I can't be trusted at all, in general."

"I'm okay with that."

"Yeah, today you are. We'll see how you feel tomorrow."

"Wait. We'll see tomorrow because you think I'm flakey and change my mind a lot, or we'll see tomorrow because you've done something tonight that I'm going to be pissed about when I find out about it?"

"Maybe both," Wade said, and the teasing tone didn't keep Jericho from believing there might be truth in his words.

"I can't believe you accused *me* of not doing things the easy way," he grumbled, relaxing back into the pillow that did maybe still carry a little of Wade's scent. They were both silent for a moment, then Jericho said, "Come over."

"Can't. I haven't done my thing that will piss you off, yet."

"It's the middle of the night. Do whatever it is tomorrow."

"It's more of a middle-of-the-night kind of thing."

"That doesn't sound good."

Wade's voice was a little husky as he said, "There are some middle-of-the-night things that are pretty damn good. I'll remind you of them next time I see you, okay?"

"And nothing you're doing tonight is going to get in the way of that? You're not going to end up in jail, or worse?" Because that was what mattered. Jericho had left the rest of the obstacles behind. His career? He'd find another. His commitment to law and order? Where the hell had that come from anyway? He'd spent the first half of his life breaking every rule he could find, and it hadn't been a problem for him, so he was reasonably confident he wouldn't have much trouble going back to that mindset. And it wasn't like Wade didn't have a moral code—he didn't kill innocent men, just like Jericho didn't, and surely that was enough. At least for a start.

But Wade wouldn't be Wade if he gave a straight answer to an honest question. "Jail? Of course not, Under-sheriff. I have no idea what you could be thinking of."

"That's not exactly reassuring."

"Well, it should be. I'm not a freestyling cowboy like you—when I make a plan, I stick to the damn plan. And I have no plans to get in trouble tonight, so everything should be good."

"Wade—" Jericho started, but then he stopped. He'd been about to whine. Better to be direct. Scary, but better. "I want to see you tomorrow. And the day after that, and the night in between. And I want to be able to touch you too, so don't say that I'll see you when you get arrested, because you know that isn't enough."

"We're not going to have a you-take-too-many-chances discussion, Jay, not when you were the one in a damn shoot-out yesterday."

"Day before yesterday," Jericho corrected, but Wade just snorted. "You know what I'm saying. You—you need to be careful, okay?"

A pause, and then Wade said, "Yeah. You too."

Jericho wanted to argue that Wade needed to be significantly *more* careful than Jericho needed to be, but he didn't get the chance, because he heard voices in the background and then Wade said, "I have to go. Take care of yourself." Then the line was dead.

Jericho was left lying alone in bed. He thought about Wade hearing about the shoot-out and not knowing whether Jericho had made it through, and groaned. It wasn't—what? Wasn't workable. Wasn't acceptable. Jericho wasn't going to spend the rest of his life worrying about Wade's safety. Wade had decided it the other night in the parking lot, and Jericho decided it right there in bed: In the future, if Wade was going to be in danger, then Jericho would be right beside him. Keeping him safe, hopefully, but at least doing something, being there for whatever happened, good or bad.

If Jericho had known where Wade was right then, he would have gone. Wade wouldn't have appreciated the interruption to whatever business he was conducting, but that would have been too bad.

But Jericho had no idea where to go. He didn't know what Wade was doing. He didn't even know where the son of a bitch lived. As usual, Wade had all the information, all the power, and Jericho was helpless. *Damn it.*

So he stayed in bed, but he didn't sleep for a long time, and when he finally did drift off, his dreams were restless and filled with blood.

CHAPTER 6

Coffee.

Jericho let his eyes drift shut as he leaned against the office wall and lifted the mug of salvation to his lips. It was morning, and Wade hadn't been brought in to the station, so that was something.

"Rough night?" Hockley's familiar voice asked from close beside him.

"Do you guys pay us when you drink our coffee?" Jericho asked. "We've got three times as many feds as locals working out of this building, and you all make yourselves at home. I know we bill you for the space and the photocopier, and I know you get our reception services for free, which is bullshit. But what I care about is the coffee. Do you all pay us for that?"

"If I were paying, I'd expect something better than this crap," Hockley said, and Jericho opened his eyes in time to see the agent grimacing as he filled his mug.

"Looking for a more robust blend or a subtler roast? Or is it the brewing method that's the problem? You're a French press guy, I bet."

Hockley raised an eyebrow in Jericho's direction. "You don't want to drink a good cup of coffee?"

"I drink coffee for one reason only, and it isn't the taste."

"It's good that homosexuality is gaining social acceptance; it'll be truly valuable for gay people to develop their aesthetic appreciation of the finer things with help from their heterosexual brothers."

Jericho snorted. "I swear, being straight is wasted on some straight men. You have the freedom to just grunt and swill caffeine without any extra effort, and you still decide to care about all that worthless crap? Total waste."

"Good coffee is not worthless crap," Hockley said with a prim sniff. Then he glared down at his mug. "Not that you could be expected to appreciate that if this is all you've got to choose from."

"You found anywhere in town yet that sells coffee you like?" Jericho asked mildly. He was getting ready for a speech about outsiders and being judgmental and maybe he'd even riff off into something about twenty-first-century hipster consumerism, but then he was distracted by a cluster of new arrivals climbing the stairs. "Shit," he muttered, and Hockley turned to see what he was frowning at.

"It's okay," Hockley said. "Kay's got it under control."

He didn't sound completely sure, though, and from the smug expression on Jackson's face as he ushered his entourage of local politicians into the central office, something non-Kay favorable was definitely going on. Jericho set his mug down on the counter.

"Hold on," Hockley warned him. "You're not going to demonstrate Kay's strong leadership by acting like an overprotective jackass."

"I am getting really, really tired of being told to do *nothing* about things," Jericho growled back at him.

"Too bad. It's Kay's call; she'll let you know when she wants you to—to be you."

Jericho glared at him, but didn't say anything more because Kayla had come out of her office and was walking toward the visitors, and he wanted to hear what she said.

It turned out he didn't need to strain his ears, because when she spoke it was in a voice loud enough to fill the room.

"I think everyone's probably aware of what's going on by now," she announced, "and I know it's becoming an unwelcome distraction from the work we should all be focusing on. So to tidy this up once and for all: I have been asked to resign from my position as sheriff with the understanding that my under-sheriff would step in and take over for me. I have refused this suggestion. As far as I'm concerned, the matter is now closed." She turned to Jenny Taylor, the county commissioner, and said, "Anything beyond this is on you."

To her credit, Taylor didn't look too enthusiastic about what she was doing. Still, she stepped forward, a file folder in her hands, and said, "We've been gathering names for our recall petition, and we're close enough that we're confident we'll have no trouble completing the requirements. With that in mind, we wanted to give you one last chance to step down—"

"May I see the petition?" a strong voice rumbled, and Special Agent Casey rumbled across the floor, his one good arm outstretched toward the documents.

Jericho glanced at Hockley, but the man didn't seem alarmed by the development. "This a plan?" Jericho hissed.

Hockley smiled enigmatically but didn't answer.

Taylor handed the file to Casey, uncertainty now clear in every line of her body, and there was silence throughout the room for a moment as Casey scanned the documents. Then he said, "What's all this about an FBI investigation?"

Taylor stared at him, then turned to Jackson, then back to Casey. "Into corruption? Former Sheriff Morgan?"

"I'm the ranking FBI officer in this region, and I'm unaware of any public information about such an investigation." He glanced around the room at his agents with dramatic flair. "Has anyone released *any* information about a corruption investigation involving former Sheriff Morgan?" After the barest pause he handed the file back to Taylor and said, "You should check your sources."

Hockley sipped his coffee and raised his eyebrows at Jericho before whispering, "Turns out the FBI wasn't too happy to learn that someone had been talking to outsiders about work they wanted to keep confidential. They have no interest in seeing a disruption to the local constabulary in the middle of their crisis."

That was when Montgomery spoke up. "DEA's been in Mosely for over a year, and we've seen no evidence of corruption from Kayla Morgan."

Good that it had been Montgomery, not Hockley, Jericho mused. Then he felt the light touch on his ribs and straightened up. His turn? "I've been sorting through old files since I got here," he announced, hoping he was playing his part right. Had everyone else been prepped for this? Why hadn't he been prepped? "No signs of anything suspicious having to do with Sheriff Morgan." He paused, then added, "And for what it's worth? I came back here to work with Kayla—I came back because she asked me to. If she's not on the job, neither am I."

A mountain shifted somewhere on the stairs, and Garron came into view. "If the sheriff goes, I go," he rumbled, crossing to the middle of the room and finding a spot to stand behind Kayla, his massive bulk making everything seem unmovable and unchangeable.

There was something theatrical at work, and maybe Jericho had been a bit too quick to disavow his gay stereotypes earlier, because he loved this scene. He started walking at the same time the other deputies did the same. Meeks, back at work for the first day since the shooting. Watson, taking a break from writing up his endless string of traffic tickets. Every piece of beige polyester in the room was in motion, all of them coming to stand quietly behind Kayla.

And she looked touched enough that Jericho felt that this last bit, at least, hadn't been staged. She must have set up the support from the federal agencies; she'd been politically savvy enough to get elected in the first place, after all. And she'd certainly have known she could count on Jericho to speak up; when had he ever been able to keep his mouth shut? But the deputies had surely been a wild card.

Now, with her team assembled, she calmly told the visitors, "You can keep working on the petition if you think it's the best way to serve the people of Mosely. But you can't waste any more of my time with it. Do it or don't do it, but don't bring it into my station again." And with that she turned her back on them. "We've got work to do, people!" she called to the rest of the room. "Sorry for the distraction, but don't let it throw you off."

Casey nodded his impatient agreement. He'd done what he had to in order to maintain the organization that supported his work, and that was all. Fair enough.

Montgomery was cool enough to turn away as well, although he was hiding a smile. Garron probably hadn't smiled since before Jericho was born, so he just stood there, grumpy and menacing, as the band of citizens exchanged glances and then meekly headed toward the stairs. Jackson followed them, his face stormy but his mouth mercifully shut. The other deputies were grinning ear to ear, and Jericho felt a surge of affection for them. They were kids, but they were good kids.

"That was fun," he told Hockley. "But it might have been nice if I'd had some idea what the hell was going on."

"Would it have been?" Hockley asked. "You generally seem to prefer spontaneity over planning."

"I prefer that *everyone* be spontaneous," Jericho replied. "But if there has to be a plan, I want to be in on it!"

"I'll keep that in mind for the future." But Hockley's attention was on Kayla. When she glanced in his direction he lifted his coffee mug in a little congratulatory toast, and Kayla grinned back at him, and Jericho's stomach twisted with—jealousy? Really?

Of the relationship, he realized. The openness. They were being subtle enough for a professional environment, but they were on the same side, sharing a victory. Kay's victory, but it wasn't a loss for Hockley, so he could celebrate with her. Would there ever be a situation where Jericho and Wade could do the same thing?

"I need to quit my job," he told Hockley, who frowned at him.

"Not until this shit with the recall is over. You threatening to quit if they fire Kayla isn't going to do much good if you already *have* quit."

"But if I'd already quit, at least they wouldn't think they'd be able to talk me into stepping up."

"And that would just make Jackson even more rabid to get Kayla out, if he knew you weren't around to fill in." Hockley shook his head and spoke with authority he absolutely didn't have. "No. You need to give her time to get things under control."

Jericho raised his eyebrows, sipped his coffee, then said, "I'm thinking about becoming a master criminal. The two careers aren't ethically compatible."

"You? A master criminal?" Hockley shifted around so both he and Jericho were looking out at the bustling office, their backs against the coffee counter. "Nope. Wouldn't work. You'd be busted inside of a week."

"What? Who's going to bust me? You? Give me a break."

"Jesus, Jericho, do you actually think you have it in you to be *remotely* subtle or crafty? You do okay as a cop because you've got power and legitimacy on your side, so when you bumble into something you can generally bluff or shoot your way out. But as a criminal? Hell no. Just because we haven't busted Granger doesn't mean we wouldn't bust you." Hockley half turned to face Jericho. "It's entirely possible you'd do something clumsy enough that we'd be able to get at Granger *through* you." He paused for another moment, then nodded. "I think you're right. I think you *should* quit your job and become a criminal."

"What about sticking around and helping Kay out?"

"Kay's a big girl—she can take care of herself. You need to do what's right for *you*. Life is too short to let it pass you by."

Jericho frowned. "I wouldn't be that easy to catch."

"No, of course you wouldn't. We'd be helpless in the face of your villainy."

"It's not like I'm *stupid*."

"That's an interesting turn of phrase. Because I would definitely say that you're not stupid, overall. But at the same time, it often does seem very much *like* you're stupid. I mean, from the outside, watching the things you do—I can see how someone might reach the wrong conclusion about your intelligence."

Jericho wished he'd never started this conversation. "Well, you're never going to catch Wade." Then he frowned. "How come you didn't tell me Mike DeMonte got killed?"

Hockley's tone was a little too casual as he said, "I don't think that information has been released to the public yet. Where'd you hear it?"

"I know a guy who knows a guy. My question is, why didn't I hear it from you? We were talking about Mike yesterday morning; yesterday afternoon he got knocked off. But it wasn't something you thought I'd want to know about?"

"It's a delicate situation," Hockley said, and Jericho stared at him.

"Shit. You haven't told *Kay*?"

That was the end of Hockley's false nonchalance. "I *can't* tell Kay," he hissed, and turned his back to the room as if worried someone might read his lips. "I can't put her in that situation!"

"You think she might tell her dad," Jericho said, realization dawning. "Or she might not. And either way, she's screwed. It's the same thing as before, when you were first investigating him. If she told him, he might change his strategy and retract any confessions he's in the middle of, and that would mean she'd betrayed the people's trust."

"And if she doesn't tell him, she's betrayed her father," Hockley finished. He shook his head. "It can't stay quiet for long. But with all this militia shit going on, nobody in the press is paying attention to anything else, so the story hasn't leaked." He frowned at Jericho. "It hasn't leaked *widely*. There's a meeting this morning; the lawyers are going to offer the ex-sheriff a deal based on his confessing to certain charges."

"But if he doesn't take the deal, he'll probably walk. The only real witness against him is dead, and you guys don't have enough other evidence to make a case." Jericho paused, hoping to be contradicted, then sighed. "Shit."

"I don't care what the hell happens to him," Hockley said fiercely. "But I care what happens to Kay, and if she knows about DeMonte it is a lose-lose situation for her."

"Shit," Jericho said again. "So—who could she hear it from? You don't tell her, I don't tell her—the person who told me likely won't tell her, but I don't honestly know who told him."

"Fucking Granger," Hockley said. "The son of a bitch has a finger in every goddamn pie in this state. And why'd he tell you? He must have known we were trying to keep it quiet. Was he hoping you'd tell Kayla?"

"Kay was thirty feet away from us when he told me. If he'd wanted her to know, he could have told her himself." Jericho caught himself. "Assuming he's where I got the information from."

Hockley didn't even bother to respond to that. "Might just be one of his games. Maybe it's more fun to torture you about whether to tell her instead of just telling her directly."

"Maybe," Jericho admitted. "But I don't think so. He's— I don't know. Do you think Kay's dad would have anything on Wade? If Wade thinks he does, then Wade would find a way to get this information to him directly—he wouldn't take the chance of me not telling Kay or Kay not telling her dad. He'd have too much to lose if Morgan testified against him. So—" *So, what?* "So if your meeting this morning goes smoothly, it means Morgan doesn't have any dirt on Wade, so Wade didn't see a need to pull his fat out of the fire. Sound right?"

"And if the meeting tanks because Morgan knows he doesn't have to make a deal? I'm going to assume it's because Granger *did* tell him, and it's going to be yet another reason for me to lock the bastard up until he's old and gray."

"You can try," Jericho said, but he wasn't really feeling the bravado. Had his big mouth just gotten Wade in trouble? "He was surprised last night. Surprised I hadn't already heard about the killing. I don't think he was faking it, so maybe he *didn't* know it was a secret. I mean, he knows a lot more than he should, but he doesn't know everything." He hadn't known Jericho had survived the shoot-out. "He might not even know you guys are trying to bluff on this one."

"He might not have known *before* he talked to you. But if you told him you didn't know, he'd start to wonder why."

"Well, for Christ's sake, Hockley, maybe you should have fucking *told me*, and then I *would* have known and I wouldn't have told him I didn't."

Maybe Hockley had an answer to that, but Jericho never heard it, because that was when the simmering activity in the FBI section of the office boiled up into an explosion of movement. Agents came pouring out of the conference room, pulling on their jackets, checking their service weapons, and heading for the stairs.

"Another damn ambush?" Jericho wondered out loud, but the energy was different. There was no panic, here, only purpose.

"Militia's heading to Helena," one of the agents told them as she waited for the bottleneck to clear at the top of the stairs. "Five vans left Tennant's ranch, and all the out-of-staters are moving down too. They're staging an illegal protest at the capitol building."

"And the FBI needs to be there for that?" Jericho queried, but she was already gone.

"Maybe they're going to make some arrests," Hockley said. "That'd be good. Apparently the guys we've got downstairs are pulling the POW thing—name, rank, and serial number only. Hopefully some of the new ones won't be quite as dedicated to the cause. A little less discipline would be useful about now."

Kay wandered over to join them, looking about as bemused as Jericho felt. He asked her, "Does this seem right to you? It's a pretty huge de-escalation, isn't it? Military-style ambush one day, killing three feds, and a couple days later they're going to march around holding signs?"

"I assume the FBI agrees with you," Kayla said. "They think something big's going to happen."

"We could go down," Jericho suggested. "It's not our case, but we could still—"

"We have work to do here," Kayla told him, as he'd known she would. She really wasn't much fun.

"Maybe we could plant some bugs in the conference room while the FBI's gone," Jericho tried. "Hockley, you DEA boys got anything like that lying around? Sheriff's department might be able to come up with two Styrofoam cups and a long piece of string, but they'd probably notice that."

Kayla stepped behind Jericho, put her hands on his shoulders, and shoved him gently toward his office. "You have paperwork. You have files to review. You can go do a foot patrol if you want, do more of your vague poking around. If all else fails, then, yes, you should go check to be sure Mr. Williton isn't trapping his neighbors' cats."

Jericho took a couple of steps, then half turned and said, "It was my vague poking around that made Sam Tennant get in touch with me, you know."

"So go do some more of it. But do *not* go down to Helena." She squinted at him. "And don't even think about going out to the compound. Just because *most* of the feds are in Helena doesn't mean they all are, and they'll definitely have their digital surveillance tools set up. Plus you have no idea what their overall strategy is, and you could mess things up if you aren't careful."

"I wasn't thinking about that," Jericho retorted. "At least, not before you brought it up."

"Bad idea, Jericho," Hockley said.

"Jay—" Kayla started.

He turned the rest of the way around and grinned at them. "Take it easy. I'll be a good little boy and do my paperwork. Go, team!"

Well, he'd have paperwork on his desk, and in a minimized window on his computer screen. But he'd mostly be scanning the internet, looking for news out of Helena. Trying not to think about Kay's dad having his meeting, and how things would be different for Kayla depending on how things went. Damn it. If Morgan knew the feds had lost their witnesses, he could refuse to deal, and the whole thing would just go away. Kayla's career wouldn't be destroyed when the feds finally released the details of whatever Morgan confessed to, Jackson would have to crawl back under his rock and shut the hell up, Jericho could quit his job and move on with his life . . . and a corrupt cop would get away without any punishment. Shit.

Jericho couldn't get involved. *Wouldn't* get involved. It was too late, anyway. The meeting had probably already started, and Jericho had no secure way to get in touch with Morgan, no way that wouldn't likely be picked up by the feds. He couldn't send a warning, even if he wanted to, and he really wasn't sure he did. So for once it was actually good to be ineffective.

He tried to go back to the internet. Hundreds, maybe thousands of militia members and supporters expected to converge on the capitol, some already there. Strong law enforcement presence. Traffic snarled, police and news choppers overhead. Jericho checked the time. The Mosely FBI had left forty minutes earlier and had a few hours more before they'd get to Helena. They weren't going to get there before the big event, whatever it was. But that was what the FBI were best for, anyway: investigating and mopping up. It wasn't like they were equipped for crowd control or any real action. They'd shown that pretty clearly the other day when they'd been ambushed. So let them go rushing down to the city.

He stared at the screen. The other day had been an ambush. That had been smart. The militia had set a trap and they'd sprung it with deadly effect. Sure, they'd lost some guys, but—what had Wade said? The militia members weren't stupid. They'd known how things would go down at the ambush site, more or less. They could have jumped in their vans and driven away well before police reinforcements arrived, but they hadn't done it. They'd wanted to be arrested.

To be martyrs, or at least to get maximum attention. To have a big, spectacular trial that would give them an audience for all their antigovernment bullshit.

Okay, but then why the protest? Why go to all the trouble of turning Sam Tennant and his family into virtual hostages if the next step involved abandoning the compound and heading down to Helena? Had they changed their strategy? If so, why?

He stood up and headed for the door of his office at the same time as he pulled out his cell phone and set it dialing. The main room was deserted, the first time Jericho had seen it totally empty since he'd arrived in town. Hockley, Montgomery, and Kayla were in her office, and he stepped inside just as his call was answered.

"Is something going on?" he said into the phone. "Something besides Helena."

"I don't know," Wade answered cautiously. "Do you have reason to believe something is?"

"I'm not playing, Wade. I need to know this. If you've got intel, I need to hear it. Because—" Because why? And why the hell had he come into Kayla's office first, before he'd had this conversation? Well, maybe because it was easier to just think it through out loud, all at once, with everyone listening. "If anyone knows about setting up one event in order to distract police attention from a different, more important event, it's you." He looked at the others in the room, frowned, and added, "Allegedly."

Then he regrouped. "I'm trying to understand this militia shit, and I can't see why they'd change tactics. Guerilla warfare was *working* for them. I mean, they got caught, but we all pretty much agree that they wanted to get caught, and they took out three feds at the same time. So why go from tactics that work to a totally different approach? Why announce their damn intentions on the damn internet, setting up a huge damn target on themselves down in Helena? Why would they do that, Wade?"

Wade was quiet for too long, then said, "I'll call you back," and hung up.

Which left Jericho with no answers and three people staring at him, waiting. "He's going to call back," Jericho said. "But I'm not wrong, am I? I know, Kay, I'm supposed to stay out of it, but . . . this doesn't feel right at all."

"And Wade Granger is going to help you feel right again?" Montgomery asked with a bit of an eye roll.

"You're welcome to try too, big boy, but I honestly think Wade's got a better chance of getting the job done."

"Okay," Kayla said quickly. "Jericho's got a point. I mean, we need to be careful, but you're not wrong, Jay—this does feel like a strange shift in their strategy."

"The problem is we don't know what intel the FBI is working with," Hockley mused. "They may have rock-solid reasons to know Helena's a real thing, a real threat."

"It's not out of the question that there could be a real threat in Helena *and* a real threat up here," Jericho said. "We don't have an accurate number for how many out-of-staters have moved in over the last couple days. The motel's full of media guys, or at least it was, but it's good camping weather and there's millions of acres of empty forest around here to hide in. If a few thousand show up in Helena, how many does that leave to cause trouble somewhere else?"

They sat for a moment, then Kayla leaned forward in her chair, focused on Hockley and Montgomery. "We need more information. You guys aren't FBI, but you're feds and not currently under investigation, so you've got an edge. Get in touch with whoever you can and try to discover what the FBI knows. Don't be shy about making people aware of our concerns. Jay, talk to the deputies in the field; tell them to play it safe and to communicate *anything* suspicious back to us immediately. I'm going to call the state troopers, the school, and the radio station to advise them of a possible situation. We all report back here as soon as we have any intel to share. What am I missing?"

"Nothing I can think of," Jericho said, and he headed for the door, Hockley and Montgomery on his heels.

Downstairs, Garron listened to Jericho's suspicions with his usual grumpy calm, then picked up the phone and started making calls. Jericho didn't ask who Garron was contacting; he just got on the radio to the deputies in the field. There were only two cars out there, one deputy in each, and he gave them a lecture about being careful and taking off at the first sign of trouble, then sent them out to scout a wide perimeter around the Tennant compound.

Then he stepped outside and stood on the front steps, gazing out at the town. The sheriff's office was at the west end of Main Street, only a few two- and three-story buildings between it and the wall of trees that marked the edge of town. Everything seemed calm.

This was all probably an overreaction, and that was fine. There was nothing wrong with being cautious.

He saw the pickup truck from a few blocks away, coming from the east. It was driving faster than it should have been, but that wasn't exactly rare in Mosely, and there weren't many pedestrians to worry about. It came closer and actually seemed to speed up a little, and years of training flashed through Jericho's mind. Explosives. Trucks ramming through roadblocks, pipe bombs, snipers. It was all from Afghanistan, not Montana, but did that distinction apply anymore?

Then he saw the driver and began to relax, at least until Wade drove the truck over the curb and up onto the battered lawn, jerking to a stop only a few feet from Jericho and the steps. There was none of Wade's usual languid grace as he threw his door open, jumped out, and jogged around the hood of the truck, his face set in an expression Jericho had never seen before.

"They're on their way *here*," Wade said. His gaze shifted to something over Jericho's shoulder, and Jericho turned to see Kayla, Hockley, Montgomery, and Garron striding out of the building, clearly drawn by Wade's dramatic arrival. Wade spoke to Jericho, but loudly enough for the others to hear. "You were right. The bullshit in Helena's a distraction. The real attack is coming here; they want to break their boys out of your jail. They think it'll be a huge victory, the sort that will show everyone the feds aren't all-powerful. They'll show that they can fight back, and other people can too."

It made sense, in a horrible way. "How many?" Jericho asked. "How soon?"

Wade's attention was all on Jericho, then, and for a moment only the two of them mattered. "Too many," Wade said, his gaze intent and almost desperate. "Too many, and too damn soon. You need to get the hell out of here, Jay. This isn't your fight."

"How many is *too many*?" Kay demanded, stepping up beside Jericho. "I need details, Wade."

"You need to get your ass out of here, is what you need," he told her, but she didn't move, and he shook his head in disgust. "The vans that left Tennant's ranch heading for Helena were empty, or just had noncombatants in them. The fighters stayed in the barn where their heat would blend in with the cattle and wouldn't show up on infrared."

"Why would there be cattle in the barn at this time of year?" Jericho asked.

"Good question," Wade said with a shake of his head. "Maybe if the FBI had any ranchers working for them, someone would have asked that. As it is? No one asked."

"Where are you getting this information from?" Hockley asked. He stepped forward to stand beside Kay and looked as if he was resisting the urge to slap a pair of handcuffs on Wade. Possibly they'd never spoken before without Wade being under arrest.

Wade directed his answer to Jericho. "Sam Tennant's cousin is Serissa Gowley, and she's been working days out at the ranch, cleaning up after the newcomers. I talked to Larry Winston who's tight with Serissa, and she got a message to Sam. He managed to give me a call."

"And he's used you as a conduit to Jericho in the past," Hockley said. "This came far too easily, too quickly. He knew what you were going to do with the information he gave you; Sam Tennant is setting us up."

"Sam Tennant is scared shitless," Wade retorted, finally looking Hockley in the eye. "He's a big talker, but he didn't want to attack the feds, and he sure as hell doesn't want to storm the county jail. His whole mission has been to support local power against the feds, not go to war with people he grew up with."

Wade turned back to Jericho. "I'm not stupid, Jay. I'm not being fooled, and I'm not lying. This is going to happen. All the guys from the compound, plus some extras on the way. The fringe people are down in Helena, but the hard-core fanatics? They're still up here, and they're coming to town. Soon."

"Give me a number, Wade." Kay's voice was tight. "And a timeline. What have you got? What *details* have you got?"

Wade frowned as if her question was an unnecessary distraction. "I'd guess forty or fifty well-armed men. They've got a few Humvees too, the real military ones, not the civilian knockoffs, and two of them have turrets. I never got close enough to see what they were carrying up there. On the ground they've got grenades, explosives, automatic weapons—what you'd expect from an invading army." He was back to focusing on Jericho as he said, "It's too damn much. You need to evacuate this building and call for—I don't know, the National Guard? You need to call for whoever the hell it is who handles shit like this, because it is way the fuck beyond your pay grade and you know it."

"I'm calling," Kay said, holding her phone up as evidence. "We're getting help."

"Great," Wade nodded toward the truck. "You want me to drive you, Jay, or you gonna take your own car?"

"Wade—"

"No," he said. "No, there is no fucking chance I'm letting you stay here. You hate your goddamn job, and now you want to die for it? No. Get in the goddamn truck."

Jericho turned to Kayla. He wasn't sure what he was looking for—not approval, not entreaty. Maybe just reality.

And she gave it to him. "I'm the sheriff. The people of Mosely County elected me, and I swore to uphold the laws. I won't let them down." She shrugged, but the nonchalance was clearly put on for his benefit. "You've been trying to resign for a while. And you were never elected—you never asked for the public trust. So things are different for you, and if you want to offer your resignation now, I'll accept it."

So there it was. Her quiet acceptance gave him permission to walk away and go find a beach with Wade. It was tempting for about half a second, but then he shook his head "Wade, I ca— There's a point where *won't* becomes *can't*. You know that. I can't walk away because I *can't*. Not—not if I still want to be me on the other side of all this."

"Do you still want to be *alive* on the other side of all this? Fifty well-armed men. Sam said they were leaving the compound when he called me; the commotion of them packing up was what he used as cover. So they're going to be here *soon*. These are federal prisoners; the feds might be borrowing your jail, but who the fuck cares? It's their problem."

"I took an oath."

"Fuck your oath!" Wade roared. The volume seemed to startle even him, and he blinked hard before repeating the words at a lower volume. "Fuck it. You don't care about this job. You don't care about the damn oath."

"You're right," Jericho admitted. "I don't care about the job. And you were right before when you said there isn't much black and white in the world; most things are shades of gray. I don't like that, maybe, but I get it." Wade tried to turn away, but Jericho leaned in and waited until their gazes met again. "But this *is*. There are rules that can be bent, and there are rules that can't. These assholes ambushed fed— No, wait, it doesn't matter that they were federal agents, it matters that they were human beings going out to ask some questions and make sure people were safe. They weren't a threat, and three of them died because some losers with guns wanted to make a point. And now some other losers with guns want to make another point by busting them loose? Fuck, no, Wade. I can't stand back and let that happen. Not because I'm a cop, but because I'm a human being."

"Stand back today and I swear I'll *help you* track them down afterward. The odds are against you now, but once the feds are here, you'll be on the strong side again. We can tidy the whole thing up later; we'll catch them all again, and it'll be good as new."

"You think they haven't got escape routes planned? Through all these trees, all these mountains? I spent too damn long in Afghanistan trying to track the enemy through mountains and trees—best terrain in the world for someone trying to disappear. The border just makes it all that much easier. They cross the line, hide out up there in someone else's forest and mountains, and then cross back down when they're ready to cause more trouble. Ready to murder more people who were just trying to do their damn jobs. It's not right, and you know it."

"Fuck what's right. Fuck *every goddamn thing* that isn't you and me. I'll leave with you this time, I swear I will. Get in that truck with me and we'll drive." He stepped closer, lowered his voice. "We won't look back. It'll all be brand-new, just you and me. No more cops and robbers, no more games." His tone was level, but his eyes? Oh god, his eyes. Jericho had never seen Wade like this, never seen him so open, so honest. Never seen him beg. And he was doing it in front of two DEA agents, people who'd never seen any weakness from him before.

He was doing all that, and still Jericho had to say, "I can't go."

Wade stumbled back as if he'd been slapped. "You *can*," he said. Another step back. "You can leave anytime you want to. You just don't want to." He was almost wild now, like he sometimes had been when they were kids and everything was too damn much for him to understand. Back then, Jericho had been the one to soothe Wade through times like this, or at least to go wild along with him until they were both ready to calm down; now Jericho was the one causing the pain.

"Wade—" Jericho started, but Wade was already moving. Around the hood of the truck into the driver's seat, and then a bouncing, jolting acceleration over what was left of the lawn. His tires screeched as he turned too sharply on the pavement, and then he was heading down the street, away from the station. Away from Jericho, who stood dumbly and stared after him.

Wade was gone.

Was this how Wade had felt when Jericho left so many years ago? This empty? This betrayed?

This is good, Jericho told himself. Wade was safe, and that was good, and it was nothing but selfishness that made Jericho feel otherwise. Wade had survived this long because he was an expert at self-preservation, so of *course* he wouldn't let himself get dragged into a suicide mission.

"No, we don't have corroborating information," Kayla was saying into the phone, and he tried to drag himself back to the current situation. "But it makes sense, doesn't it?" She paused, and then said, "That was a completely different situation. The bikers were— Yes, I called you for help with them as well." She was breathing hard, clearly trying to keep her cool. "I know it was a false alarm that time, but I'm not sorry I called you—there was enough intel for the risk to be at least possible, and—" She stopped, listening, and shook her head in frustration. "Yes, but—" She closed her eyes, maybe praying for patience.

Hockley and Montgomery had their own calls going on, and Jericho let the conversations wash over him. He didn't need to pay attention to the details, not when the general responses would be the same. The real battle was going to be in Helena; there'd already been one false alarm this summer, and nobody had time or manpower to deal with another one; Mosely was on its own.

Jericho was on his own. Wade had *left*. If Jericho didn't come out of this—and he wasn't going to come out of it, not when he was one of a handful of barely armed officers facing a heavily armed platoon—then that would be the last conversation he and Wade ever had. The yelling at each other was okay. They'd always spent a fair bit of their time yelling. But Wade had walked away. Had he ever done that before? Had he ever turned his back on Jericho when Jericho hadn't already done the same?

Jericho forced himself to think about the practical side of the upcoming battle. M4s. The FBI had taken the ones actually involved in the shootings, but the department had a couple of extra; they were in the squad cars. Ammo. They had enough of that.

Strategy? What the fuck was the strategy going to be?

He looked at the building; it was brick, sure, but not the kind of stronghold police stations in bigger cities had been turned into. No barriers to keep vehicles from driving right up the front, no fortified areas inside. The holding cells were reached through the front doors, or through a service entrance around the back. The front doors were metal, but not specially reinforced. They'd be easy to blow through if the invaders were as well equipped as Wade—*no, don't think about him*—as intel suggested.

Jericho's phone rang as the other three were on their second or third round of desperate phone calls, and he saw Meeks's name on the display. He kept his gaze on Kayla and lifted the phone to his ear. "Crewe."

"We have activity out here, Jay!" Meeks's voice was tight and high. "I'm out on Coldcreek, about six miles out of town, and there's a—a—I don't know, a damn *invasion* coming past me!"

Jericho's gut churned. It was real. It was happening. "Meeks has visual confirmation," he told Kayla without lowering his own phone. "Meeks, give me numbers, descriptions—what are you seeing?"

"Oh fuck!" Meeks shouted. Jericho's grip tightened on the phone as unintelligible noises crackled in his ear.

"Meeks!" Jericho yelled. There was crackling, but no words. Jericho told Kayla "Something happened. They're six miles out of town, on Coldcreek. He said it was an invasion, but I'm not getting anything more out of him." He tried not to let his imagination fill in the blanks in that summary, and Kayla's grim expression made it clear he didn't need to speculate.

"Forty or fifty well-armed men," Montgomery said, "and we're already down one deputy."

"I've called everyone in," Garron rumbled, "but most of the boys live out of town. It's going to take a while for them to get here. I'll send a couple of them around to check on Meeks."

Kayla kept yelling into her phone, and Hockley and Montgomery's conversations took on new urgency. Jericho looked at Garron. "Yeah. Send two deputies to Meeks. One town ambulance should go out there too, but it needs to take the long way around. Coldcreek. Have the other ambulance stand by here. And give me the keys to the armory." There were too few weapons in the room for it to really deserve the name; he probably should have called it the closet. But it was what they had.

By the time he'd returned with an M4 for everyone and all the ammo the department had, the others were off their phones.

"We're getting a chopper," Kayla said flatly. "ETA half an hour."

Half an hour was too long, and they all knew it. And a single chopper? It would help, certainly, but it wouldn't turn the tide.

They were quiet for a moment, staring at each other or down the road in the direction the militia would be coming from, and then Kayla said, "This isn't a DEA issue. Hockley, Montgomery—you should go, and make calls from somewhere safe. We need contact with the outside, and you two can—"

"No." Hockley glanced at Montgomery, saw whatever he needed to, and turned back to Kayla. "We're law enforcement. We stand together."

Jericho's mind raced, trying to sort out the tactics. Five of them, lightly armed, against forty or fifty attackers. He asked Garron, "What have we got in the evidence lockup? Is that grenade launcher still here? Anything else that would be useful?"

Garron shook his head slowly. "FBI shipped everything off to their labs." He gestured to the M4s. "This is the best we've got. If we had time, we could—" He broke off, looking over Jericho's shoulder.

Jericho turned and looked down the street toward town. It was the wrong direction, and it wasn't a military strike coming toward them, it was a pair of tow trucks, each pulling a trailer full of—

"Those are the junk bins from Scotty Hawk's place," Kayla said almost experimentally, as if she were trying the words out to see if they made any more sense when spoken aloud.

The tow trucks were close enough now that Jericho could recognize Scotty's bulk behind the wheel of one—and something loosened in his chest, then tightened again, when he saw Wade driving the other. Wade didn't even glance over, and he was yelling something into his phone as they drove by, but . . . he was there. He was doing something weird, but that was okay.

And then Jericho clued in. "They're blocking the road," he told the others. "There's just one way into town from this direction, and they're going to block it. We need to get a few more vehicles in place behind those bins, because Humvees have a lot of power. Hopefully they'll leave the tow trucks, so that'll be some good weight, but—"

He was interrupted by a rumble from down the road and turned again, this time to see a huge dump truck crawling along Main Street. It was taking up both lanes of the road and nearly sideswiped a couple of parked cars as it came.

"That's from the old equipment yard." Kayla sounded amazed. "From the mine. I had no idea it could run anymore."

Jericho didn't want to think why Wade would have known the truck's status, what nefarious scheme it might have been part of, but it was good to remember who he was dealing with. "Wade has the roadblock under control," he said. "That'll get the enemy out of their armored vehicles and away from their turret guns, and it'll slow them down. That's a start. But we're still going to be outgunned and outmanned."

"Not by as much as you'd think," Garron said, and Jericho followed his gaze back toward the town.

More trucks were arriving. A stream of them, these ones civilian pickups, but each driven by someone Jericho recognized. He glanced over to see Wade jogging back from where he'd left the tow truck, a heavy bag slung over his shoulder and his deer rifle in one hand, an M4 in the other. He didn't look in Jericho's direction, just shouted at the new arrivals. "Gather up over here to get instructions!"

Mr. Appleby was one of the first to arrive, rifle in hand.

"No," Jericho said, turning to Kay. "Shit, Kay, we can't ask them to do this."

"You think we need to be *asked* to defend our own damn town?" Mr. Appleby barked. The kindly shopkeeper was gone, replaced by a hard-eyed, if somewhat gray-haired, warrior.

"I don't know what you've heard," Kayla said, loudly enough that the gathering crowd could hear her, "but we're expecting a fairly intense attack. This isn't something that's going to—" She stopped and grimaced. "It's not going to peter out like the biker thing did. At least, I don't think it will. This is going to be a fight. People are going to die. The enemy may have explosives—"

"So do we," Wade said, and he shrugged the bag off his shoulder and lowered it to the ground. "I raided the toy store. Now, where do you want us set up?"

"You don't have to—" Kayla started again.

"Are we just going to pick our own spots, then?" Nikki demanded from the middle of the crowd. She was carrying Eli's Remington. No. *Her* Remington. "Or are you assholes going to come up with a plan?"

There were more fighters pulling up, jogging over with rifles in hand, and Scotty Hawk and a couple of other men were swaggering back from the roadblock, obviously satisfied with their work. Montgomery and Hockley were back on their phones, speaking urgently to people who were almost certainly too far away to be any use. Kayla looked at Garron, then Jericho. "You *said* it wasn't about your job. You said you were here because it was the right thing to do. If I listened to it from you, I should listen to it from them. And you're the one with the military background, so this is your show. Where do you want them?"

He wanted them home safe. But if he couldn't have that— "You don't have to be here. This doesn't have to be your fight. But if you're here, please work from as much cover as possible." He waited, not sure whether to hope people would stay or go. When the only movement was in the form of new arrivals, he scanned his eyes over the crowd. "Raise your hand if you've ever been active military, ever seen action." Six men and one woman raised their hands, and Jericho nodded. He might have hoped for more, but seven out of twenty-something was pretty good. "Okay. Each of you take two or three others with you."

He squinted down the street. "There are five buildings between here and the forest. Split up. Get up onto roofs or upper-floor windows. Don't take unnecessary chances, just harass the enemy and try to pin them down. We've got air support coming in." Not enough, of course, but maybe enough to scare the attackers off. "Time is on our side. If we can slow them down, we're doing well." He tried to think what he was missing. "Watch for them trying to get inside the building or around into the alleys. North-side shooters, keep an eye on the south-side buildings, and the other way around. Cover each other from across the street. They've probably got grenade launchers, and maybe worse. If you see anyone with—" how to describe all the possible variations of weaponry they could be facing? "—with anything bigger than a standard rifle, that person is *everyone's* first target. And if you see anything like that pointed in your direction, you run the hell away and try to get as many walls between you and the shooter as you can."

There had to be better instructions he could give. If he had more time, he could work on tactics, set up a plan. But as it was? "You don't have to do this. You don't need to be here. These guys are coming in to bust some of their friends out of jail, not to invade the town permanently. You don't have to be here, especially not if you have kids."

"Kids make it *more* important to be here," Johnny Flear said. He was quiet, determined. "I don't want my kids growing up in a world where they think outlaws can attack the sheriff's station and get away with it. We elected the sheriff; she represents *us*. So if someone attacks her, they're attacking us too."

Jericho couldn't argue with the sentiment. So he just said, "Once the chopper arrives, or any kind of backup, stay out of it. You might look like militia to people who don't know better, and we don't want our reinforcements taking shots at you." He took a deep breath. "Okay, go. Find somewhere safe to shoot from."

"Stay in touch," Wade said. "The radio station will relay instructions, or if you don't have a radio, check Twitter. Hashtag Mosely."

Jericho frowned at him. "Seriously? There's a hashtag? Is that how you got everyone here so fast?"

"No," Nikki said, checking her weapon and scowling at Jericho. "He used the school phone tree. Everyone who gets a call when school is canceled got a call for this. And then we contacted a few extras."

"Jesus. You guys take your snow days pretty seriously."

Nikki gave him a dead-eyed stare, then turned to the others. "Let's go. I'll take the farm-supply building."

And they went, scattering across and along the street like an army of toy soldiers gathered from too many different games.

Jericho watched them go. "From a traditional law enforcement perspective, I probably should have focused on only shooting in self-defense, and maybe said something about respecting property," he said, mostly to himself. Then he turned to grin at Kayla. "If I play my cards right, I might be able to get fired after all this."

Wade glared at him, acknowledging his existence for the first time since his return. "If you're still alive after all this, you are absolutely quitting your fucking job." Then he nudged the gear bag with his foot. "There's some shit in there that might help keep us alive. At least long enough for me to kick your ass."

CHAPTER 7

Jericho was crouched over, sorting through Wade's loot bag, when he heard the rumble of approaching engines and the warning yells of the fighters closest to the barricade. "I say we start in the street and retreat back to the jail if we have to," he said to Kayla.

"No," Wade said. Apparently he didn't share Kay's faith in Jericho's tactical judgment. "Fuck that. We don't care if the assholes get to the jail. I mean, *I* don't care about any of this. But *you* don't care if they get to the jail. You only want to be sure they don't get the prisoners out of town, right?"

"Well, okay," Jericho said cautiously. "I mean, best-case scenario, the bad guys would lock themselves up in a few free cells and sit there until the feds come to collect them. But I don't think that's likely, do you?"

"No," Wade said. "I think they'll fight their way in, spend some time blasting their boys free, assuming they haven't got keys or some tool to override the locks, and then clear out. Since they're going to know this route is full of hostiles, they'll take another path. *That's* where we should be waiting for them."

"So what's the other path?" Jericho wasn't ready to challenge Wade's understanding of the patterns of villainy; the plan definitely made more sense than Jericho's version. But how was it going to work in practice? "They'll make a run for the border? Maybe they'll abandon their vehicles; too easy to track them. So eight miles to Canada, mostly forested—" He stopped and frowned. "Straightest line is through those back fields, then right into the damn school yard. We've got the building on lockdown, but is that enough? Are these fuckers going to want to take a few hostages for insurance?"

"I wouldn't be surprised," Wade said, and slapped a clip into his rifle.

"So we run a rolling retreat," Jericho said. "We start on the street, fight our way back to the building, *don't* go inside, and set up an ambush between the station and the school."

"I think we can arrange a few surprises for them inside the sheriff's station too," Wade said. "I'll take care of that while the rest of you keep an eye on the street and shoot anyone who tries to rush my schedule. Sound good?"

"Are you seriously going to blow up my station?" Kayla asked.

"Parts of it." Wade almost smiled. "I deserve to get *some* satisfaction out of this, don't I?" He glanced toward the barricades, which still showed no signs of movement, and then toward Jericho. "You'd better appreciate this shit."

"I absolutely do." And right there, in front of God and the town and the DEA and everybody, Jericho stepped forward, caught the back of Wade's neck in his hand, and pulled their faces together for a fast, hard kiss. "And you can do anything you want to my ass, kicking or otherwise, after we get out of this."

And there it was, finally, Wade's smile. Just a flash, but enough. "I'll hold you to that, Junior," he said, and then he turned and grabbed the gear bag in one fluid movement, lifting it to his shoulder as he jogged up the stairs into the sheriff's station.

The *crack* of a hunting rifle rang down the street, and then another, and another. The townsfolk with military experience would probably be the first ones able to break the taboo against shooting at another human being. But from the sound of things, they weren't acting alone.

Jericho turned to see militia members scrambling around the barricade, searching for cover as they took fire from the buildings on either side of the road. They were three or four hundred yards away and moving targets: he wasn't likely going to hit much, but he could at least draw some fire away from the civilians. So he found cover behind a pickup and looked through his scope.

He was vaguely aware of the activity around him. Extra townsfolk were arriving, armed and ready, and Kayla was directing them as well as she could with all the chaos. Garron had found a pickup of his own and was setting himself up, and Hockley and Montgomery were each behind one of the big pines in the front of the station. There were still shots ringing out from down the street. Mosely was being invaded, and Mosely was fighting back.

Jericho took a deep breath, let it out, and snugged the butt of his rifle in against his shoulder. It was too familiar, and too strange, to be back in a war zone. *They're not people; they're targets*, he told himself, and he gently squeezed the trigger.

He saw the man—the *target*—jerk, stagger, and fall. No time to think about it, thankfully, as he scanned for his next shot. There were at least five of the invaders on the ground, and hopefully more bodies hidden behind the dump truck. But there were still a lot left and they were moving purposefully—no signs of panic.

You guys should turn around and go home. You don't need to do this today. Or ever. Nothing you're doing needs to be done. Turn around.

But the militia didn't seem to pick up on Jericho's message. They had found cover and were firing at the buildings, little clouds of brick dust puffing out wherever their bullets hit the walls. The fighters in the buildings were no longer at the windows, Jericho was happy to see. But that left the path essentially clear for the invaders, and they obviously knew it.

He saw the tube of the rocket launcher and had his rifle raised before his brain fully recognized what it was. "RPG!" he screamed so loudly something tore in his throat.

No sight line on the asshole holding the launcher, not from where Jericho was, so he broke cover, firing as he went, hoping fate would guide a bullet to his target. As soon as he was moving he saw the muzzle flashes from the barricade, at least a dozen enemies taking aim at him. *Shit.* He had to keep going, had to keep working his way across the road so he could get a bead on the guy with the rocket launcher. The launcher was pointed right at the upper windows of one of the buildings, and would have enough power to take out half the wall and anyone taking cover behind it. Jericho needed to stop it, but he couldn't find a line, he wasn't going to—

The barricade exploded, an eruption of smoke and fire and twisted metal. The man with the RPG was lost in the middle of it all.

Jericho dove for cover, bewildered, mind racing as the thunder of the explosion rolled over him. He wanted to be relieved, but what the hell had just happened? Had it been the rocket launcher, misfiring or misdirected? Was there actually some power in the universe smiling down on Mosely that day?

He flopped onto his back and glanced toward the sheriff's office. That was where he saw Wade, standing on the front steps watching Jericho with a beatific smile. There was a little box that could only be a detonator in his hand, and as he caught Jericho's eye he mouthed, *Surprise.*

"Jesus Christ," Jericho said. The higher power wasn't in the sky above them, it was Wade fucking Granger, which seemed perfect somehow. Wade had left explosives in the truck, and he'd detonated them.

It had to be over, didn't it? Maybe the enemy wouldn't have lost that many men in the explosion, but they would have lost *some.* And it was a clear sign that they weren't coming up against villagers armed with BB guns. They had firepower, but so, thanks to Wade and his illicit arms, did Mosely. The militia had to see sense now. Whoever was in charge would have to order a retreat and make a plan for another day.

Then Jericho saw movement through the smoke. The explosion had been strong enough to shift the dump trunk a few paces backward, and it had practically destroyed one of the junk bins that had been the first line of the barricade. Now, through the destruction, a Humvee was rolling forward. There was a heavy gun in the turret, a live body behind the armor ready to man it.

"Fuck," Jericho said, to himself and anyone else within earshot. The explosion had still been a good thing; it had taken out the damn rocket launcher before any townspeople had been targeted. But the militia was taking advantage of the opportunity. He jogged toward Wade, tagging people's shoulders as he went and yelling, "Rolling retreat. Shoot as you go, but *go!*" He didn't want to think about the damage that turret gunner could do if he let loose on the flimsy civilian pickup trucks.

Wade was waiting near the doorway of the sheriff's station. Now that his life was in danger, there was none of the emotion he'd shown earlier; he seemed as calm as if he were waiting in line for a movie he didn't particularly care about seeing. "This is going better than expected," he said as he watched the Humvees approach. "I assumed we'd all be dead by now."

"The explosives helped. You didn't think to mention that to me?"

Wade looked almost hurt by the suggestion. "I told you I had toys. But giving you the details would have ruined the surprise."

Jericho turned, and together he and Wade sprayed a few shots at the approaching Humvees. Kayla had marshalled her late-arriving troops behind cover across the street from the station, and they were taking shots as the opportunities presented themselves. Jericho hit the button on his shoulder-mounted radio—it wouldn't work for anyone but Kayla and Garron, but at least it was something. "Stay where you are," he directed. "Set up some cross fire and make the fuckers work for every yard."

"Roger," Kayla said. "I've got about ten guys over here, and more are still coming in from out of town. Lots of hunting rifles."

"Roger," Jericho said, and kept moving.

"What did you get set up inside?" he asked Wade as they found cover behind one of the squad cars in the parking lot. It felt wrong to let the invaders enter the building, but that was the strategy they'd decide on, and it was too late to change it. Hockley and Montgomery were already in the parking lot, covering the front door from behind one of the unmarked sedans. Garron was with Kayla. He was too big, too slow, to be part of the mobile strategy.

"Couple tripwires, a kilo of C-4 each. Won't have sight lines, so I didn't use anything I'd have to trigger from a distance."

The Humvees were coming faster now, the gunners spraying bullets in all directions. Jericho hunkered down, trying not to imagine one of those bullets finding his flesh. He'd been shot before, and he really, really hadn't enjoyed it. So it was best not to think about any of that and just keep his mind on the job. The militia members who couldn't fit in the Humvees were jogging along with them, using them for cover; it slowed the procession down a little, but not enough. Jericho found a target and squeezed the trigger, refused to look at the man as he fell, and shifted to find someone else to shoot at.

"They might go back the same way they came in," Wade said, sounding like it was all an interesting academic puzzle. "Now that they've cleared a path, they won't want to leave their vehicles behind unless they have to."

"Shit." If someone was going to change a plan, he wanted it to be him, not the enemy. He found a target and fired. *Shit, shit, shit.* "We still have to cover the other exit." They couldn't take a chance of letting the militia get to the school. "And Kayla's got more guys coming in." He glanced over and saw a familiar shape looming beside Kayla—her father had arrived and he'd brought his gun. Must have been in his truck when he'd gone to his meeting. "They'll take care of the front way."

"Okay," Wade agreed easily. He took a shot, then another.

"Wait." The Humvees were pulling up in front of the building, now, jumping the curb and rolling over the lawn just as Wade had done. "You got any toys left? Maybe enough to disable the vehicles?"

But Wade shook his head. "I've got a few grenades. But they won't do much against armor."

Hockley and Montgomery were firing, now, doing a fairly good job of keeping the militia away from the front door, but then the turret gun turned their way. They pressed themselves flat as the car they'd been crouched behind jerked and jumped and spat bits of metal from its newly perforated surface. There was a bit of a ditch at the edge of the lot, and it would give good protection even against the heavy gun, but there was a patch of open ground between it and them.

Jericho fired at the Humvee, but the turret was well-protected, of course. The DEA sedan was being torn apart, Hockley and Montgomery were flat on the ground, maybe dead already. But, no, Hockley raised his head, looked over at Jericho—and then Jericho felt movement behind him. Wade was standing, throwing, flopping back down. A grenade.

The explosion wasn't as big as Jericho might have wanted, but it shut the turret gun up, at least temporarily. He and Wade both peered around their cover vehicle and squeezed off a few shots, and then Wade was up again, throwing again, and this time when he dropped down he jerked his hand at the agents, directing them toward the ditch.

They scrambled as the second explosion thudded through the air and were safely behind the wall of earth before the noise was gone.

And there, in the middle of it all, Jericho's phone buzzed in his pocket. He had a nearly hysterical moment of wondering if it was a telemarketer, but when he pulled it out Kayla's name was on the display.

"I quit," he said into the mouthpiece.

Her voice was tight, almost a gasp. "Okay. Me too."

That wasn't what she should sound like. "You okay?" he demanded. "You hit? Why are you using the phone?"

"Ricochet hit the radio. You believe it?"

"Just the radio? The radio's strapped to your shoulder, Kay!"

"My shoulder too. But I don't think it's bad." She might even be telling the truth. "Nice aim from Wade—boy's got an arm. But I think he just took out the gunner, not the gun itself. They'll be shooting again in no time. And they're keeping men in the Humvees—not everyone seems to be going into the building."

Keeping men in the Humvees. So some of the militia were planning to make it out on the road. But that didn't mean all of them would be.

"Can you handle this side?" Jericho asked. "We've got some time while they're getting inside, and then getting into the holding cells ... can we get the road reblocked?" He checked his watch. It had been less than ten minutes since the attack had begun; help was still far away. "Wade and I can handle anyone who goes out the back door."

"Sure," Wade said with an exaggerated nod. "Sure, we can handle them. Just the two of us. No problem."

"You got a better plan?" Jericho demanded.

"Yeah—we could *leave*."

"A plan I can go along with?"

"I can send a team around the long way," Kayla said in Jericho's ear. "They can rendezvous with you at the school. Sound good?"

"*That* is a better plan," Jericho said, and ended the call. "She's sending guys to meet us at the school."

"I'm sure that'll make all the difference." Wade nodded toward the front door of the building. "Looks like they're going to blow things open over there. The lock slowed them down, but it hasn't stopped them."

There was something about the way he said it that made all of Jericho's senses switch to high alert. Something that let Jericho know that Wade wasn't going to let the militia's plan go off quite as tidily as they might have expected. Sure enough, Wade calmly pulled his detonator out of his pocket, twisted the dial on top, and depressed the trigger. Then he smiled, not flinching at all as the front steps of the office were lost in a cloud of smoke and fire. Jericho flattened himself against the shaking ground just before the noise rolled over him, the deafening thunderclap followed by the pings of debris hitting the parked cars.

Jericho rolled onto his side and stared at Wade. "You said you wouldn't have sight lines. You said you were out of—"

"You didn't like my 'run away' plan. Now don't tell me you don't like my 'blow shit up' plan, either, or my feelings will be hurt."

Jericho stared at him for a moment, then shook his head. "I fucking *love* your 'blow shit up' plan. Is there more of it?"

"Maybe."

"I love you." The words were out before Jericho knew they were coming, and he panicked a little. "Your plans. Your explosions. Your—" Wade was still so calm, but looking back at him with a light in his eyes, a light that Jericho never, ever wanted to extinguish. "Your you," he finished. "I love you."

"And you're not just saying that because we're both about to die?"

"Maybe I am. But that doesn't mean it isn't true."

"Well, okay, then." Wade smiled, then turned back toward the front of the station, raised his gun, and fired, possibly at nothing. "They're going inside, most of what's left of them. They'll either be slow 'cause they're watching for traps, or they'll be fast and getting themselves blowed up. So we've got a bit of time. You want to cut around back and find a good path?"

And clearly Jericho was just as much of a flip-flopper as Wade had said he was, because now that Wade was on board, Jericho wanted to bail out. He wanted to take Wade's hand and drag him away from all the mess, all the violence and death and even the explosions, although those had actually been pretty cool. Kayla had sent a team to the school, and that would probably be enough. If it wasn't enough, was it really Jericho's problem? Hadn't he done his part? Wasn't it time for a beach somewhere?

"Junior!" Wade said, his voice just a little sharp. "Let's go. Bad guys. School. Remember?"

"Yeah," Jericho said. "Sorry." Maybe if there hadn't been a school involved, he could have left. But a building full of kids, two of whom shared his blood? No, he couldn't walk away from that. Damn it.

"Keep your head in the game," Wade scolded, and he started off toward the fields, jogging cautiously from car to car as he worked his way through the parking lot.

Jericho followed. This was Wade's show now. Hell maybe it had been all along. Maybe Jericho could save himself a lot of trouble if he stopped thinking so much and just did as he was told.

He managed to cling to that philosophy as they headed around the back of the station. Wade's smile was bloodthirsty when they heard a muted thud from the other side of the brick wall, and he said, "Tripwire number one. They'll know to be looking now, so the second one might not catch 'em. But they'll be slower." He glanced over. "We probably have time to stop for a quick drink, if you want."

"Tempting. Your call."

"Ah," Wade said as they made their way across the street and through the pedestrian gate of the school playground. "We're having a visit from cooperative, tractable Jericho. You have any idea how long he'll be around for?"

Jericho stared across the field toward the one-story school building. Two pickups were pulling onto the tarmac, men and guns in the back of each. One of the trucks was driven by Mike Darby, who'd graduated high school with Jericho and Wade and now had five kids enrolled in the elementary school. Of course he was there.

The other truck, though? Ex-sheriff Morgan was behind the wheel. Kayla's dad, who'd been a self-righteous asshole not only when Jericho was a kid and had deserved it, but also after Jericho's return. And the bastard had been selling information to criminals while he was on the job and even after he'd retired. Hell, he'd been selling information to *Wade*. "I think cooperative Jericho is on his way out," Jericho said. "I think we're about to have a visit from stubborn, pissed-off Jericho."

"Well, he's always been one of my favorites," Wade said, and he nudged Jericho forward with his shoulder. "Come on. Let's go make a plan."

CHAPTER 8

I t was overly generous to call "get between the militia and the school and shoot at the bad guys" a plan, but Jericho liked it when things were kept as simple as possible. He didn't like it so much when the defenders spaced themselves out, taking whatever cover they could find, and he found himself huddled behind the same dumpster as the ex-sheriff.

"Push that end around," Morgan ordered. "We'll have better sight lines."

So tempting to disagree, but the benefit was too damn obvious, so Jericho did as he'd been told, then cast his mind around their environment to find an order *he* could give. He almost told Morgan to go double-check that the door to the school was locked, but the bastard would probably tell him to do it himself. And he was a lot more spry than the old guy; it made sense for him to be the one moving out of position. So he jogged over, rattled the door, then jogged back to the dumpster and dialed his cell, feeling like an idiot. What the hell kind of battlefield had cell reception? Still better than using the damn hashtag. "We're in position at the second location," he reported when Kayla picked up. "We've still got air support incoming?"

"Air support and ground support," Kayla confirmed. It was reassuring just to hear her voice, even if she sounded a bit strained. "There was a significant increase in interest once we started reporting the body count."

"I'll bet. You have eyes on the front door?"

"Yup. Nothing yet."

That was likely good. No, it was definitely good. The longer the militia was inside the station, the better the chance that air support would arrive, and tracking the bastards would be much easier with an aerial view. "The new guys know about the weaponry we're looking at?" Jericho asked, thinking about an RPG taking out a low-flying chopper.

"Affirmative," Kay said. "Hockley and Montgomery are with me, and they're reporting back. We've got a fucking news crew over here too. They've been filming the whole thing from the motel window, and they keep trying to get closer."

"Okay," Jericho said. It was all okay. There was a hell of a mess on Main Street, and there might be some civilian injuries. Of course there would be. But over all, this could have been—

He saw the beginnings of movement over at the fence line. Maybe a dozen men, and if that number included the four prisoners it meant Wade's booby traps had done their jobs well. The militia were staying low and slow, but they were coming. And as he stared out toward them, fighting to determine numbers or weaponry or anything he could use, he found himself distracted by something much closer. A small red light, a tiny black box attached to the side of the dumpster he was hiding behind. Wires ran from the box up to the insides of the bin.

"The dumpsters are wired!" he roared. "Get away from the dumpsters! Take cover!"

He'd been turning as he yelled, but not fast enough. *Nothing* was fast enough. It was like the world had been submerged under water or Jell-O, everything happening far more slowly than he wanted it too. Everything except his senses, which were suddenly hyperalert. He could see the man at the fence with the black box in his hands, could see the antenna stretching out from it, could see the bastard looking over, seeing them, and trying to decide whether to blow the bins now or wait for a better chance. He could see Wade and Mike Darby sprinting away from their dumpster, heading around the corner of the building. And he could see Morgan scrambling, almost falling, then recovering and scrambling for the cover of the nearest pickup.

Then he saw nothing. He heard nothing. He was maybe aware of pressure—weightlessness, beyond his control, and then a moment of thudding pain, and then it was back to nothing.

Jericho came to in a cloud of dust and confusion. He was in a battle; that much was familiar. He couldn't hear much, just the dull roar of his blood and a muffled, distant version of gunfire and yelling. His ears were damaged, and they weren't the only part of him in trouble. Maybe he should just let his eyes shut; they wanted to shut.

But he forced himself to roll onto his side, then fought to keep the dizziness under control. He blinked a few times, trying to make sense of the scene in front of him. Twisted metal, not the sandy beige of a tank or a Jeep, but mid-blue, with rusty patches—dumpster. *School. Militia. Wade!*

He squinted through the falling grit. There were bodies—and parts of bodies—there were two pickup trucks, both blown over onto their sides, legs sticking out from underneath at least one of them. The school—he looked behind him: the windows were jagged holes but the walls were standing, and the lockdown drill involved moving all students to interior rooms. The kids should be okay, as long as nobody got inside. But Wade. Where the hell was Wade?

He'd been wearing black and gray, as always. Jericho pushed himself to his feet, using the wall for balance, and screamed, "Wade!"

There was no answer. There was also no more gunfire, not even the distant thuds his damaged hearing had given him. No one left for the militia to shoot at? Was that what the bastards thought? *Was it true?*

Wade. Where are you?

No, Jericho couldn't think about that. He couldn't let himself fall apart.

He stumbled through the debris, wishing he had something to wash his eyes with besides his tears, and finally saw movement. Maybe a hundred yards away, the remaining militiamen were jogging through the field, heading for the school.

Jericho didn't care what their strategy was. He didn't care if they were planning to take hostages or just start killing, whether they'd hole up in the building and force the feds to negotiate or just grab some kids and run for the border. They'd had the school in mind when all of this started; they'd had the foresight to come by ahead of time and plant the bombs in the dumpsters. So this was what they wanted?

That was too fucking bad, because they couldn't have it.

If these fuckers had hurt Wade, then they couldn't have *anything*.

Jericho patted his body experimentally and found his M4, still on its strap but slung way around his back. He pulled it to where it belonged.

The weapon felt right in his hands. And it felt good to start moving, not too steady on his feet, but improving as he went. He shifted laterally to the men, and they were out in the open, while he remained hidden by the debris and the dust. His first burst caught the leader, his second the man behind them. He was mowing them down like the psychotic weeds they were, and he knew his lips were drawn back in a feral snarl.

He ran out of ammo just as he reached one of the overturned pickups, pulled another clip from his vest, and slapped it into place. He'd taken out at least three of them, maybe four. Where were the rest now? Creeping toward him, or into the school?

His ears were still useless, and that was a nuisance. He was bleeding too, from at least a few shrapnel wounds and possibly a new graze earned on his most recent efforts. No time for first aid, and fuck it anyway. He didn't want to help himself, he wanted to hurt others. He wanted to destroy anyone who'd hurt Wade.

So he scrambled to the far end of the pickup, darted his head around for a quick look to be sure the path was clear, then eased around the corner. Dizziness hit him, and he had to lean on the twisted tailgate of the truck. He refused to pass out. This wasn't over, not yet.

He had to make a decision. He had no way of knowing where the enemy was—stalking him or ignoring him and heading for the school. They were disciplined enough to sacrifice themselves for the cause—they wouldn't be coming after him for revenge, he didn't think. But they weren't stupid, and they wouldn't want him at their back as they tried to do whatever they were planning to do inside the building. They'd be coming for him.

And they'd expect him to be hiding. He was one man, and there were still at least four of them, maybe more. They were better armed. They weren't injured. Anyone with sense would be retreating and finding cover.

Jericho tested the stability of the pickup, then hooked his fingers over the top of it—the side, under usual circumstances—and pulled himself up. It was a wide-bedded dually, almost eight feet off the ground, and for a moment he thought he'd lost too much blood and wouldn't have the strength to lift himself. Then he remembered himself and Wade at the cave in the forest months earlier, climbing the cliff, wrestling at the top. *Wade. Goddamn it, Wade.* Jericho grunted a little as the edge of the truck rubbed against sore spots on his torso, but he was up.

Slithering forward, staying low, keeping quiet. He wasn't the prey; he was the hunter. Searching, stalking—and discovering.

The men had split up. Four of them left, as far as he could see, two of them following Jericho's route around the front of the truck, the other two cautiously working their way around the back. And both teams were divided even further, one partner cutting the corner from up close, the other providing backup from thirty feet out. That made sense, if they were the aggressors. But it wasn't nearly as good of an idea when they were on the defensive.

Jericho groped inside his vest for the clip he'd emptied moments before and looked toward the school. It was hard to guess how much noise was needed—his own hearing had been okay until the most recent explosion, but these guys had been inside the sheriff's station when Wade's—*shit, no, don't think about Wade*—when the booby traps had gone off. So he threw the empty clip somewhere it would make enough clatter for them to hear it, hoping they wouldn't realize it was too obvious.

It worked. The pair closest to the school exchanged glances with each other, nodded, and changed track so they were facing away from Jericho's truck toward the school.

The other two were trickier, but not by much. A simple sit-up, ignoring the streak of pain across his belly, and two shots into the head of the man farther away. His partner saw him fall and assumed Jericho was on the far side of the truck, shooting out at him. As soon as he moved past the tires Jericho rolled off the truck behind him, popped two bullets into the man's back, then turned to face the men who'd been heading for the school.

He should dodge, and he knew it. He should find cover, play it smart, live to fight another day. But Wade hadn't shown up. Wade was—he wasn't something Jericho *ever* wanted to think about, and there was only one way to keep himself from doing that. So he didn't dodge. These bastards had come to his town and ripped it apart, come to his *life* and ripped it apart. He roared as he sprinted toward them, firing as he went.

One man fell just as the first bullet hit Jericho in the thigh. He took one last step, landing on his good leg as he fell, and his aim was off, his balance, maybe even his vision. But he was close enough now. His body jerked as another bullet hit him, and the shock and blackness closed in. But before it overtook him he saw the man's throat disintegrate, saw him fall backward and away. He saw enough, and let his eyes close as his body toppled to the tarmac.

CHAPTER 9

You're an asshole.

And later, *You're an idiot.*

Such an asshole.

After another indeterminate period, *I'm going to kick the shit out of you.*

Jericho's inner voice had always been unkind to him, but it had never actually threatened violence before, and it tended to be more specific about Jericho's failings. Was this the afterlife, then? A new world, with an even meaner, vaguer voice yelling at him?

"Stupid son of a bitch."

Wait a second.

Jericho fought to open his eyes. Yeah, he had eyes. He had a damn body. He tried to sit up, panicked when he couldn't, then realized he was squeezing warm fingers in his left hand while a somehow-familiar bulk leaned over him and pressed on his chest. "Stay still, asshole. The doctors spent a lot of time on you. Don't fuck it all up now."

Jericho knew that voice, knew that scent, knew that *hand*. "Wa . . ." he tried. Well, that wasn't quite right.

"Shhh." For the first time, Wade sounded almost gentle. "You're okay. You're an idiot and I'm going to kick your ass, but you're okay. Stay still."

"Wh . . ." Jericho honestly couldn't say whether that had been an attempt at Wade's name again, or one of the *w* questions: Where, Why, When, and definitely What the fuck?

Wade apparently decided it was the last one. "You're in the hospital. You got us both blown up and then you got yourself *shot* up. Remember?"

Did Jericho remember that? All he could truly recall was the gaping emptiness in his chest where Wade was supposed to be. And now Wade was back? "De . . ." Well, this one was worth working a little harder for. "Dead?" he croaked.

"You sound terrible. And using that voice to say words like that? Jesus, Jay, I'm an invalid. You can't be freaking me out all the time—not cool." He squeezed Jericho's fingers. "I already buzzed for a nurse, but I'm gonna go hunt one down and carry her back here, okay? She'll— I don't know, give you ice chips or knock you out so I don't have to listen to you or something."

But when Wade tried to extract his fingers and Jericho squeezed tighter, trying to hold on, Wade didn't leave. And a moment later, there was a brush of softness against the back of Jericho's hand. A kiss. "You scared the shit out of me," Wade said, his words muffled and soft. "We aren't doing that again, Jay."

Jericho wanted to say okay. He wanted to say more than that. A lot more. Instead, he faded away, back into the hazy world of drugs and injury, and he stayed there for quite a while.

The next time he came to—or maybe not the exact next time, but some other time—he wasn't clear on linear progressions right then—he heard Kayla's voice. And this time when he tried to open his eyes they worked, basically. Stung like he'd been caught in a sandstorm, didn't show him anything but way too much light and some general, moving shapes, but his eyelids opened. He tested his left hand, and Wade was still there. He tried to turn his head in that direction and set off an explosion of pain and dizziness and nausea. Jesus. He wanted to see Wade, but not *that* much. Feeling him was probably enough. Hearing him would be nice. "Hey," he grunted.

"You're an asshole," Wade responded.

There'd been enough of that. "Wh? Why?"

"Kay showed me the fucking security tapes from the school—I get a tiny bit knocked out and you go fucking Rambo? I mean, I was feeling you when you got up on the truck—that was smooth. But you should have kept your ass up there! What was all this charging around like a kamikaze bullshit?"

How to explain? And *whether* to explain? And did he really need to explain?

"Couldn't find you," he managed, pleased that his voice, although thick and gritty, was at least coherent.

"Too fucking bad," Wade said, his own voice muddier than usual. "If you can't find me, you still have to take care of yourself, you big fucking baby."

It might be better to just feel Wade, rather than see *or* hear him. Jericho squinted down toward the end of the bed. "Kay? You all right?" There seemed to be too much white on her torso, not enough beige. She was in uniform, but wearing a sling?

"I'm okay," she said. "You scared us, Jay, but you did a good job. Nobody made it to the school. The prisoners didn't escape. Nobody escaped—we've got fourteen injured militia members, but the rest of them—"

"The rest of them should have stayed the hell out of Mosely," Wade said, and there was the promise in his voice that if anyone ever messed with his town again, they'd meet the same fate. A bit hard to reconcile that with the man who'd planned on finding a beach when this all started, but Wade had never worried too much about being self-contradictory. So Jericho wasn't going to worry about it either.

"Our side?" Jericho asked. He wasn't sure he wanted to know. Might be easier to just fade back into drug-land and not hear about the consequences of the battle.

"A lot of injuries." Kayla's voice was tightening up, and Jericho regretted the question. He wasn't the only one who'd be feeling bad. "Some of them fairly serious. A couple amputations. Meeks is just down the hall, and he's in better shape than you." She paused, took a deep breath, and then before she could continue, Wade broke in.

"The only deaths came at the school," he said. "You, me, and Mike Darby are the only ones who came out of that alive."

Mike Darby. He had all those kids, so that was good. But— "Oh shit." Jericho wished Kayla were closer, wished he were fitter so he could hug her. Her dad had been at the school. "He was— Damn it. He was protecting his town. His people."

The beige and white blob nodded, maybe a little too hard. Maybe as if it was trying to shake tears back into its head.

And then Wade let go of Jericho's hand, and the cool clamminess of the skin left behind made it clear this was the first time they'd been out of contact with each other for quite a while. The black and gray blob moved to the foot of the bed, the beige and white blob took half a step back, then half a step forward, and then the gray blob's arms were around the beige and white blob, and everything was as good as it could be expected to be.

The truce didn't last long before Kayla pushed herself away and Wade returned to Jericho's side. They were all quiet for a moment, and then Kayla spoke, her voice strong again. "You have a head injury, Jay, so you might not remember. But in case anyone asks—we deputized everyone. Do you remember that? It was a quick thing, not really a ceremony at all, but everyone who got injured—if their insurance doesn't cover them, it's okay because the department's insurance will, because they were properly deputized at the time. Do you remember that?"

"There were white flowers." Jericho's voice was still raspy, but he was feeling better. "A huge central display, with boutonnieres for every new deputy."

"I swear to God, Jay, do not start mentioning flowers," Kayla warned. "Keep it simple. We swore them in. That's all."

"Was there a Bible? Oaths of any sort?"

"I think you probably don't remember anything that happened that day," Kayla said firmly. "Does that sound about right? Your memory is completely gone?"

He almost wished it were. "Patchy. But I definitely remember something about deputizing."

"I remember it too," Wade said cheerfully.

"No one's going to ask you, Wade." The beige blur stepped back from the foot of the bed. "Not unless things have gone horribly awry."

"Hockley's okay?" Jericho asked. His mouth was so dry he was pretty sure the skin of his tongue was going to lift right off and adhere to the roof of his mouth with his next words, but there were some questions that needed to be asked.

"He will be," Kayla said, and she was her fierce warrior self again. "He got hit late in the game. Might lose part of his leg, but he'll be okay."

Maybe Jericho hadn't needed to hear that. He remembered to not move his head, but cast his eyes down over his own body as far as he could see. Still two legs. Two arms. "Me?" he asked Wade.

"You're going to be a crabby bitch in physio for a few months, and they took out your spleen. I swear, they do that just so they can say they did something. They took a chunk of your liver too. They're probably going to eat it."

"Jesus, Wade," Kayla said, but she sounded like a mom, not a sheriff. "Nobody's eating his liver."

"She's not a doctor," Wade faux-whispered to Jericho. "She doesn't know."

Jericho's world was a surreal hospital room. But Wade and Kay were both in it, and they were almost getting along. So he had no complaints, and let himself drift away.

Things were significantly less pleasant the next time he opened his eyes. Wade was still there, so it wasn't terrible, and Jericho could see him clearly now, which was certainly an improvement. But the men standing at the foot of his bed? The men in suits, with not-that-subtle bulges to show where their sidearms were holstered?

Jericho squinted at them. "Low on douchiness, high on self-righteous bullshit. I'm guessing FBI."

"I'm Special Agent Lines," one of the men said. Lines? Or Lyons? Lions? That would be nice, if he were a special feline agent. Jericho could feel the morphine doing its business on his body and figured there was no reason to work all that hard on controlling his mind. It made it a bit easier to listen when he was picturing a talking lion. "We're going to need to ask you some questions about the events in Mosely last week."

"Last week," Jericho said. Okay, technically that could be just a couple of days earlier, if they were counting the weekend as the start of a new cycle. He turned to look at Wade, and this time it barely hurt at all. Absolutely no urge to puke on Wade's creased gray shirt.

"It's been nine days," Wade said gently. "You were pretty fucked up, so they kept you unconscious. They say you can talk to these guys, but the second you decide they're doing you no good? Like, if you have a *hangnail* and you think them being here is making it worse? Let me know, and they're gone."

Was it the fun of being in power over feds or of getting to be protective of Jericho, or some combination of the two? Did it matter? Wade was happy, and that meant Jericho was happy. "My advisor will let you know when I require a recess," he said archly to the feds. "And, while we're at it, could you clarify just which agency you're being so special at?"

The agent's pleasant expression seemed frozen. "FBI," he replied. "Yes. Now, about the incident in Mosely last week. We're asking some questions, obviously. We're going to need you to walk us through it from the beginning."

"The beginning?" Jericho asked. "Can you be a little more specific than that?"

"Whenever you think it's most relevant. We can ask you follow-up questions if needed."

Jericho looked over at Wade, then back at the fed. It was stupid. He didn't have the strength for this crap, and even if he did, there was no reason to be childish. No reason except that the citizens of Mosely had fought alone while the feds had ignored them. No reason except that citizens of Mosely were *dead*. Kay's father was dead, and he'd been a duplicitous asshole but still her father. Other citizens, probably all assholes in their own way, had also been heroes in their own way. And this fed was here *now*, when it was too late? As if he somehow had the right to judge when he hadn't been there to take part? And as if his agency wasn't going to be looking for ways to excuse their mistakes . . .

Jericho smiled sweetly. "I'd like to think it all began on the day I left Mosely, a day scented with pine needles and opportunity. But, really, to truly understand, we may need to go further back. I was born on a cool morning in early May . . ."

He kept talking for as long as he could, and then he sucked on the ice chips Wade brought him, and talked a little more. The feds probably weren't that interested in his feelings toward his fifth-grade teacher, who'd combined nurturing and torturing in fairly equal parts, but they'd stood there and listened as long as they could stand. And when they finally left, Jericho found enough voice to call out after them. "Be sure to come back tomorrow! We might get to the times I lost my virginity. That's right, I said time*s*."

He was tired. Possibly exhausted. But then Wade smiled at him, and Jericho could have stood up and walked right out of the hospital if Wade thought it was a good idea.

Instead, Wade said, "I fucking love you. You know that, don't you?"

Thankfully, Jericho no longer felt the need to vomit whenever he nodded. "I suspected; I *am* a detective. But it's nice to hear it."

"Doesn't mean I'm not going to kick your ass, though," Wade said as Jericho faded out. "Let's not get confused about that."

By the next visit from the feds, he was up and walking around. Not walking quickly or anything, but upright. Standing up made defiance just a little bit easier, not that he really felt like he needed the help.

But for their second visit, the feds brought Kayla. It had been more than two weeks since the shoot-out and she was back at work, back where she belonged, but she still looked strained and miserable.

Jericho knew why she was there, and the strategy was going to work, as long as the feds didn't push too hard. "Maybe this would go better if you asked me some specific questions," he said. Wade sighed in disappointment, but that was okay. There were other ways to satisfy Wade, and Jericho almost felt up to some of them.

"Specific questions?" Lines asked, all innocence.

Jericho had thought he had himself under better control, but something about the way the bastard said those two simple words was a little too much. So his own smile was just as innocent as Lines's, and if the fed didn't see that as the warning it was, that wasn't Jericho's problem. "I haven't watched a lot of TV lately, but I assume this has been a big deal. The feds totally fucking up, the locals having to step in and take over like we did. I assume that's been a huge mess for all of you?" He gave another smile, and Kay's lips twitched as she looked at the ceiling tiles, so Jericho knew he was on the right track. "I imagine it'd be a lot easier for you if you could find someone else to blame for this mess? Maybe someone local?" Jericho turned to Kayla. "I quit, Sheriff. I am no longer an employee of the Mosely County Sheriff's Department." He shifted his gaze back to the feds. "So I've got nothing slowing me down, and as you may have already noticed, I like to talk. I bet reporters would like to listen."

He smiled at Wade. Yeah, that beach was still in their future. But when Jericho left Mosely this time, he wouldn't be running away from anything.

"So, I'm happy to answer any of your questions. And if I see that things aren't going the way I think they should—if I see Sheriff Morgan or any other resident of Mosely taking unnecessary heat for anything they did when the feds *fucked off to Helena and left us on our own*? I'll answer questions from reporters too, and from anyone else who will listen." He smiled again, and for the first time it was a tiny bit forced. "You might not believe it to see me right now, but in general, I'm pretty fucking photogenic. I bet TV would love me." He glanced over at Wade. "Which is my good side?"

"All your sides are just fine," Wade reassured him, and it was about more than photographs, about more than any damn thing.

Jericho winked at the man he loved and said, "Yours too," and when Wade nodded, he knew they'd come to an understanding.

What that understanding *was*, he didn't really know. He didn't really care. The feds left soon after without asking any questions; maybe they'd already gotten the answer they needed to hear.

The next morning Nikki came to visit, and she brought the kids. They both greeted Wade warmly, Jericho with veiled suspicion. Elijah was interested in Jericho's bandages, at least, accepting the invitation to perch on the bed and poke at various injuries. Nicolette stood beside her mother and scowled. Still, it was touching that Nikki had made the effort, driving all the way to Missoula just to see him. Touching, but strange.

"I need to talk to you," Nikki said to Wade, and then the visit made sense. This wasn't about family-bonding time, it was about business. Crime. "Jericho can watch the kids so you and me can talk outside."

"Jericho can't handle your kids when he's at full strength," Wade replied. "It's been a lot of trouble for a lot of people to get him patched up; I can't let him get torn apart again."

Nikki snorted in disgust, but it was clear her derision was aimed at Jericho, not Wade. Still, there was a little heat left over for her business partner when she said, "You can't disappear for a couple weeks and expect everything to keep running without you. There's stuff I can take care of, but there's stuff I can't."

"It's okay," Jericho told Wade. He'd been tricked before, of course, overestimated his beast-taming skills, but surely he could manage the kids this time? "For a few minutes. And don't go far. Give me my cell before you go so I can call for backup." He looked at Nicolette. There were different rules for different animals—was he supposed to avoid eye contact with a feral child, or insist on it? "We could watch TV," he suggested.

Her snort was a near-replica of her mother's. "That TV's a piece of crap."

"Yeah, I think I'll choose a different hotel next time. You want to handle the remote?"

Wade was clearly doubtful, but he found Jericho's cell phone and handed it over. He took a few steps toward the door before turning and frowning at the kids. "Hey," he said, not loud but somehow still powerful. Both kids turned to gaze at him like they'd been hypnotized. "Jericho is *not* in charge. He's hurt, and you guys shouldn't be his problem at the moment. *I'm* in charge. And I'm going to be on the other side of that door. If he's not completely happy with the way you're behaving, he's going to call me, I'm going to come back in, and I won't be happy. Understood?"

Threatening small children. Jericho probably shouldn't have seen it as an expression of love, but he probably shouldn't do or feel most of the things he was doing and feeling, so there was no need to worry about one more transgression.

"We'll be fine," he told Wade.

Wade left reluctantly, Nikki eagerly. Nicolette didn't give any more attitude before flopping dramatically down into the chair Wade had just vacated. She started flipping through TV channels while Elijah peered at Jericho intently. Maybe a little too intently.

"What's up, buddy?" Jericho tried.

Elijah frowned back at him, but it was a puzzled expression, not an angry one. "You're my brother, right?"

"Half brother. Yeah."

"Is that like a real brother?"

"Uh, yeah, I guess. We're brothers, sure. That's just a fact." Not necessarily a pleasant fact, but he didn't need to point that out to a six-year-old. "But there are different ways to be brothers. You know? We can just be technical brothers. We have the same dad, so we're brothers, but that doesn't have to mean anything. Or we can be *real* brothers. Like, we can have each other's back and try to watch out for each other. You know?"

Elijah nodded thoughtfully, and there was a nice moment of companionship as they both contemplated their relationship. Then Elijah said, "If we were real brothers, could I shoot your gun? The big one that you killed all those guys with, not your little one."

Jesus. "The big gun isn't mine. It belongs to the sheriff's department. So you'll have to grow up and be a deputy if you want to fire that gun. And I think the feds still have my little gun. So I am currently unarmed. Sorry."

Elijah nodded sadly. "Maybe that's good. Seems like you get shot a lot when you have guns."

"Yes!" This was a breakthrough, surely. "You *are* more likely to get shot if you have guns. They make things kind of dangerous—"

"No. Not everyone. Just you. *You* seem to get shot a lot. So maybe *you* shouldn't have guns."

"Maybe I shouldn't," Jericho agreed. Maybe the beach would have a no-weapons policy, and he'd be just fine with that.

They sat in peace for another couple of minutes until Wade and Nikki returned. Nikki gathered the kids without a word to Jericho and left without looking back.

"She seemed slightly less pleasant than usual," Jericho said. "You tell her something she didn't want to hear?"

"I told her I was out."

Jericho stared at him. "Out?" Out of the closet? But that made no sense. "Like, out of business?" Wade's expression answered the question, but Jericho added, "Entirely?"

Wade shrugged, then said, as if starting a whole new conversation, "You should see the way the town's treating Kay—she's their warrior queen, their hometown heroine. Jackson has oozed back into whatever swamp he came from, and no one's interested in bad-mouthing an ex-sheriff who died heroically in defense of the community he served. So you're free too, Jay. I mean, if that whole 'I quit' thing was just for the feds, I get it, but—"

"Wade. I'm quitting."

Wade's shoulders relaxed. "So . . . I am too. No more cops and robbers. I'm done." There was a moment of silence in which they both seemed to be waiting for the lightning bolt to punish Wade for his offense against the natural order. But nothing came, so Wade added, "And that means Nikki is going to have to either find something else to do or do it all herself, and she's not too pleased with either option."

"That's it?" No lightning indicated cosmic complaints, but even from Wade, surely there should have been more. More drama, probably. More of a fight. This felt too easy, and with Wade, easy tended to mean a trap. "Will the people you work with let you walk away?"

Wade shrugged. "I think so. I've been careful, built in some safety plans and favors and whatever—should be fine. Most of the bikers are in jail, most of the militia leaders are dead or in jail—honestly, this is a good time to get the hell out."

"What about the feds?"

Another shrug. "I don't think Hockley's got quite such a hard-on for busting me anymore. Seems like saving his life wasn't quite as much of a mistake as I'd been thinking it was. And since the unfortunate incident with the evidence room, they'd pretty much have to start their case over at the beginning. I don't think they'll bother, not if they're sure I'm retired."

"What unfortunate incident with the evidence room?"

Wade's innocent look was always an excellent sign of guilt. "Oh, did I not mention that? The charges I laid in the sheriff's building—one of them just happened to be in the doorway to the evidence room. Those wire cages do a good job of keeping people out, but—" he shook his head with exaggerated regret "—they really aren't fireproof. And the sprinkler system wasn't too kind to what was left, as I understand it."

"Jesus Christ, Wade." But Jericho didn't want to fight about it. Wade's charges had taken out more than half of the militia members who'd made it as far as the office. If he'd taken out a little evidence as well? Nothing came for free, not with Wade.

"The point is, yeah, I think I can walk away from it all."

"So we're both unemployed." Maybe that was the trap. Maybe Wade thought he could starve Jericho into joining him in his criminal enterprises if there was no money coming in. "I've got savings. I never made that much money, but I live pretty cheap. As long as we don't go crazy, we can live for quite a while on what I've got."

"I've got some money put away too." There was something strange in Wade's expression as he added, "So, beach? Somewhere cheap? Or—" He stopped, and waited.

Waited for Jericho to change his mind. Waited for him to back out, or make an excuse, or in some other way make it clear that being with Wade came second, or third, or maybe even lower down the priority list. Shit. Jericho had done that. Jericho had made Wade expect that.

"Beaches are too far away," he said. "And I'm not sure about flying while I'm still a bit messed up. How about the mountains? We've got a couple months of easy weather left—want to find a tent and a mountain lake and hide in the forest for a while? Living off the land is a good way to save money."

And now Wade's silence made it clear he was looking for traps as well. Which was maybe fair, considering how many times Wade had manipulated Jericho in the past. But Jericho wanted this to be about something more than fair.

"Your call," he said. "We can get in the Mustang and drive, if you want. I don't care where we go. You didn't want to leave Mosely when we were kids, but if you want to leave now, I'll come with you. Or I'll stay with you. It's the 'with you' part that I'm focusing on, in case you didn't notice."

"I should have come with you then," Wade managed. "I was too chickenshit to do it, but I should have found the guts, and we wouldn't have wasted all that time."

"The larger world really isn't that scary, you know."

"The world?" Wade frowned at him. "It's not the world I'm—I *was* scared of. It was just knowing that you and me made sense in Mosely. But out there, with so many other options? I figured you'd end up seeing how much better you could be doing, and— I don't know. I guess I thought it was easier to not try, instead of trying and failing."

"That *is* chickenshit." Jericho didn't want to be angry, but remembering how hard it had been for him to leave? Realizing he'd had to go alone because Wade had some stupid moment of insecurity and had been too stubborn to talk about it? "Damn it, Wade, you couldn't have mentioned that to me then?"

"What would have changed? You needed to leave; I could see that. If I'd told you about it, what would have been different?"

"What's different *now*?"

Wade's grin was quick. "Well, now you're all old and shot up. Nobody but me is going to want you now."

"We're the same age, asshole."

"But one of us is a little better preserved than the other. Less damage to the upholstery."

Jericho wasn't going to take that bait. He didn't want to fight with Wade. Not yet. "So you're feeling more secure now? You'd be okay with leaving Mosely?"

"Yeah," Wade said slowly, clearly bracing himself for the inevitable.

"Okay, then." Jericho relaxed back into his pillows. "I think we should stay."

"What?"

"We should go to my place when they let me out of here—or, hell, you could actually show me where you live and we could go to your place. And then when I'm less likely to have a weird relapse or something, we should go live in the woods for as long as we can stand it. After that?" He pushed himself up in the bed, trying to look like someone who had good ideas. "We should stay in Mosely. The damn town's all messed up, and *we're* all messed up, so it's a good fit."

"The town fights when it has to, and *we* fight when we have to, so maybe we belong there," Wade mused.

"The town's got a history, but it's trying to build a future. Just like us."

"The town's about five miles off the highway and the streets are laid out in a grid pattern, and *we're*—" Wade stopped. "Well, the comparison only goes so far, I guess."

"But how do you feel about the general principle?"

"Staying in Mosely?" Wade made a face. "It's complicated, obviously. You're friends with the sheriff, who's dating the man who's spent the last couple years of his life trying to put me in jail. We're not going to be having Scrabble nights with them, if that's what you're thinking."

"It's not. I hate Scrabble."

"And Nikki and the kids are here. My mom's here. All good reasons for us to get the hell out of town."

"They are," Jericho agreed.

"The town thinks they know who we are—maybe they'll be a bit more open-minded with you since you already changed yourself once, but I don't think I should be counting on that for myself."

"Meaning we'll have even fewer people wanting to play Scrabble with us. Sounds good to me."

"Are you serious about this?" Wade asked.

It felt good to be the unpredictable one for a change, good to have Wade wondering instead of the other way around. So Jericho tried to look serene and mysterious as he said, "Maybe."

"Maybe," Wade echoed. He squinted at Jericho, then shook his head. "No. Fuck it. Why do that to ourselves? Mosely doesn't need us; it might be Mosely needs us to get the hell out so it can start pulling itself back together. And you know what else? I don't give a shit what Mosely needs. You've shed enough blood for this damn town, and I've wasted enough years here. Let's start over somewhere else. Somewhere we can be normal people."

"Normal people?"

"Build a whole new life. White picket fence, two point four kids."

"Maybe the fence," Jericho said. "But not the kids. Kids are awful. If part of your planning for the future involves offspring, we're going to have a problem."

Wade grinned. "You can't judge all kids by Nicolette and Elijah. *Our* kids would be raised right, and I'm sure they'd be lovely."

It was almost time to panic. "Is there any chance our kids could have, like, tails, and fur? Four legs probably?"

"Well, yeah, obviously. I thought that would go without saying."

"Okay, then." Jericho let himself relax again. He was about ready for a nap, and it was nice to go to sleep with total confidence that Wade would be there when he woke up. "I'm in."

"White picket fence? Mosely or somewhere else?"

Jericho thought of his struggles to speak when he'd first been coming round, thought of the questions he'd maybe been trying to ask, and realized that they didn't matter. Well, *What the fuck?* was probably always going to be a useful one as long as he was with Wade, but the others? Where, when, why, or how? None of them were important. The only one that really mattered was *who*.

"We'll figure it out," he murmured, letting himself drift further into sleep.

"We'll do it better this time," Wade agreed.

And that was enough.

Jericho had come back to Mosely for his father. Out of duty, guilt, and maybe a vague idea of making things better, of repairing at least the surface of the relationship while there was still time. Instead, he'd found Wade. He'd found Kayla. Mr. Appleby. Deputy Garron. Hell, he'd found Nikki, and the half siblings he hadn't known existed. His life had been empty, and now it was full—too full, in terms of Nikki and the kids. Little brats.

He thought about smiling, but he was too sleepy. Too content. Possibly too drugged, but mostly just happy. He and Wade had found each other. And this time they were grown men, not confused boys. This time they knew what it was to lose love, and they both knew enough to make sure it never, ever happened again.

EPILOGUE

"**M**ore fucking sand," Wade griped, looking out at the expanse of white and blue in front of them. "And we both know there are sharks in that ocean. They're coming for us. You first, probably, because you're bigger." He leaned over on the sheet they were using as a shared beach towel and let his hand wander up Jericho's thigh, edging his fingers in toward one area that would definitely be getting bigger if things continued.

Jericho calmly sipped his Piña Whatever and nodded. "Beaches are highly overrated."

They weren't, of course. The beach was beautiful, the drink was delicious, and it felt good to have the sun baking the muscles he was still exercising for therapy instead of fitness. They'd found a cabin that was remote enough, in an area that was liberal enough, for them to spend most of their day naked, in the water or on the shore. There was absolutely nothing wrong with the beach. And that was the damn problem.

After Jericho had been released from the hospital, he and Wade had spent a few days at Jericho's apartment with Jericho reclining on the couch while Wade packed the place up, making fun of whatever caught his eye. Luckily Jericho had most of his mementos, the few things he truly cared about, in storage back in LA. Although he had a feeling Wade would have been good at figuring out what was important and what was open for ridicule. Wade was good at figuring most things out.

They'd camped in the mountains for a few weeks while Jericho still had frequent medical appointments, then packed up the Mustang and headed for Mexico, Jericho telling himself that Wade's interest in the border crossing was innocent curiosity. They'd found somewhere cheap to stay, because Jericho didn't have all that much in his savings and Wade was being cagey about his own financial situation, and they'd had a good couple of weeks. Now, though?

"The sun's bad for your skin, you know." Wade frowned and ran his fingers over one of Jericho's still-pink scars. "And you're not as dark as I am. You need to be more careful."

"Also, Spanish is kind of hard to understand," Jericho contributed. He edged closer and took a deep breath of appreciation as Wade's fingers closed around his cock. "Life is easier when everyone speaks English."

Wade's hand was relaxed. Just a casual handjob on the beach— might turn into something more, might not. "Authentic Mexican food isn't as good as I thought it would be. There's not enough cheese."

They could have kept going, but there was no need. "We're bored," Jericho said.

"Perfection sucks." Wade rolled quickly, then shifted until he was hovering over Jericho, their legs entwined, their cocks lined up in happy comradeship. "The only reason I can stand you is because you're so deeply, deeply flawed."

"Is this going to be about my scars, again?" Jericho wrapped his hand around their cocks while Wade began to work his hips, slow and easy. "Because chicks dig scars. I've heard that on good authority."

"Too bad you don't dig chicks." They kissed, then, their mouths communicating as well, if not better, without words. *No, it's not too bad we don't dig chicks.*

It was all magically familiar, even with the sand and the tropical sun. It was sinuous Wade and solid Jericho, just as it had been when they were teenagers, and just as it should always be.

"I love you," Wade whispered, just as he always did when his climax was building. Just as he always should. Jericho kissed Wade, and they moved together in perfect rhythm, perfect balance, and came together with a shuddering release as timeless as the waves lapping against the shore.

Jericho stayed silent until Wade had shifted back over to his own side of the sheet, then said, "So, we're bored. And you have a plan. Are you going to tell me what it is?"

"Why do you think I have a plan?"

"Because you're you. Are you going to tell me what it is?"

Wade made him wait a little, but finally shrugged and said, "Jericho Crewe: Private Investigator."

"Private Investigator." It wasn't exactly a wild idea; a lot of PIs were ex-cops. "How do you fit in? There are background checks before you can get licensed, Wade. Hockley might not be actively trying to bust you anymore, but he's not going to cover for you. There's no way you'll get a license."

"Also, there's a written exam, and I don't like studying. I said 'Jericho Crewe,' not 'Granger and Crewe.'"

"So what the hell will you be doing?"

"I'll be doing the *real* work. The real investigation. We'll be like that TV show, where you can be the public face of the company, being what people expect a PI to be, but I'll be the one getting shit done."

"*Remington Steele*? You want us to model our business after a cheesy eighties TV show?"

"Yes. Yes I do."

"You know, I'm actually a competent investigator. I don't just have good hair, or whatever the guy from the TV show had."

"Of course you are. You'll be helpful to me. Especially with the routine cases. The paperwork. That sort of thing."

Well, they could squabble about that some other time. "Why? What makes this a good idea?"

Wade smiled at him with warmth and affection Jericho wished he could bottle. "Because we're both getting restless. We're both likely going to end up doing something that makes people want to shoot at us, sooner or later. And it's important to me that when people are shooting at you, I be there to shoot back. So, this seems like a reasonable solution. It's not completely outside the law, so you don't have to get all prissy and uptight about that. It's not completely *inside* the law—or it won't be the way I do it. So I'll be free to let my instincts take over and keep us safe. And it could be fun."

"Fun?"

"It'll have all the things you like about being a cop—helping people, getting shot, whatever—and none of the bad things—like hanging out with cops, following cop rules, being a cop. None of that. Sound good?"

"I'm not sure."

"Are you worried about having to write the test? It's cool, I can help you study. I can probably get some fake ID and take the test for you, if you want."

"You are so annoying when you're in a good mood."

Wade grinned at him. "We should do it in Montana. Not in Mosely, because I don't think there'd be enough business, but somewhere close by so we could keep an eye on the kids."

"From a distance."

"For you, that's likely best. I might sneak in a little closer now and then."

"And will you check on Nikki's business while you're there?" Jericho tried to keep his tone light, but Wade wasn't fooled.

"Not on purpose," he said, keeping his gaze locked with Jericho's. Wade didn't lie, not like this. "And if something came up, I'd talk to you about it. Just like Kay might ask you for a favor sometime and you might think about doing it, but you'd talk to me first."

Jericho let himself relax. "A PI, huh? And you'd take care of all the hard cases?" The idea was starting to grow in his mind, starting to make a place for itself in his imagination. He'd still be helping people, but he'd have more flexibility, fewer rules to follow—no bosses, no feds. No brown-on-beige polyester. "Okay, yeah. Let me read up on the requirements. Let me think about it."

Wade leaned back, satisfied.

And Jericho could have left it there, but instead he added, "You understand that I'm interested in the 'helping people' side of things, not the 'getting shot' part, right? I don't get shot on purpose."

"Of course not," Wade agreed. "You're not just hungry for attention all the time. That's not what it is."

Jericho raised an eyebrow, and then he pounced. Wade was fast, and he'd never be taken in by Jericho's attempt at trickery, so he clearly wasn't trying too hard to avoid being caught. Caught, wrestled, and pinned, Jericho sitting on Wade's chest, careful that his knees didn't push down on Wade's biceps hard enough to hurt. "I'm only looking for *your* attention. Nobody else's."

"Well, you've got it." Wade heaved his body a little, experimentally. They both waited a moment, then Wade shrugged his surrender, and Jericho slid down his body until they were lying together. "You've always had it," Wade said gently. "And you always will."

"Damn right," Jericho said, and they lay there together as the sun went down over the ocean.

Explore more of the *Common Law* series at:
riptidepublishing.com/titles/series/common-law

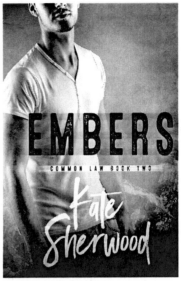

Dear Reader,

Thank you for reading Kate Sherwood's *Home Fires*!

We know your time is precious and you have many, many entertainment options, so it means a lot that you've chosen to spend your time reading. We really hope you enjoyed it.

We'd be honored if you'd consider posting a review—good or bad—on sites like **Amazon, Barnes & Noble, Kobo, Goodreads, Twitter, Facebook, Tumblr,** and your blog or website. We'd also be honored if you told your friends and family about this book. Word of mouth is a book's lifeblood!

For more information on upcoming releases, author interviews, blog tours, contests, giveaways, and more, please sign up for our weekly, spam-free newsletter and visit us around the web:

Newsletter: tinyurl.com/RiptideSignup
Twitter: twitter.com/RiptideBooks
Facebook: facebook.com/RiptidePublishing
Goodreads: tinyurl.com/RiptideOnGoodreads
Tumblr: riptidepublishing.tumblr.com

Thank you so much for Reading the Rainbow!

RiptidePublishing.com

ABOUT THE
AUTHOR

Kate Sherwood started writing about the same time she got back on a horse after almost twenty years away from riding. She'd like to think she was too young for it to be a midlife crisis, but apparently she was ready for some changes!

Kate grew up near Toronto, Ontario, and went to school in Montreal, then Vancouver. But for the last decade or so she's been a country girl. Sure, she misses some of the conveniences of the city, but living close to nature makes up for those lacks. She's living in Ontario's "cottage country"—other people save up their time and come to spend their vacations in her neighborhood, but she gets to live there all year round!

Since her first book was published in 2010, she's kept herself busy with novels, novellas, and short stories in almost all the subgenres of m/m romance. Contemporary, suspense, sci-fi, or fantasy—the settings are just the backdrop for her characters to answer the important questions: How much can they share, and what do they need to keep? Can they bring themselves to trust someone, after being disappointed so many times? Are they brave enough to take a chance on love?

Kate's books balance drama with humor, angst with optimism. They feature strong, damaged men who fight themselves harder than they fight anyone else. And, wherever possible, there are animals: horses, dogs, cats ferrets, squirrels . . . sometimes it's easier to bond with a nonhuman, and most of Kate's men need all the help they can get.

With her writing, Kate is still learning, still stretching herself, and still enjoying what she does. She's looking forward to sharing a lot more stories in the future. (And check out her imaginary friend, Cate Cameron, who writes m/f romance and YA.)

You can find Kate at:

Facebook: facebook.com/kate.sherwood.79

Twitter: twitter.com/kate_sherwood

Goodreads:

goodreads.com/author/show/3462951.Kate_Sherwood

Enjoy more stories like
Home Fires
at RiptidePublishing.com!

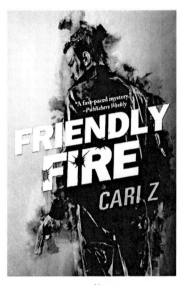

CPSIA information can be obtained
at www.ICGtesting.com
Printed in the USA
LVOW12s2046060717
540480LV00001B/86/P